Totally Bound Publishing books by SA Welsh:

Out of CTRL

Shifter Protection Specialists Inc.
Purrfect Protector

I0571309

Shifter Protection Specialists Inc.

PURRFECT PROTECTOR

SA WELSH

Purrfect Protector
ISBN # 978-1-78430-415-7
©Copyright SA Welsh 2015
Cover Art by Posh Gosh ©Copyright January 2015
Interior text design by Claire Siemaszkiewicz
Totally Bound Publishing

Published in 2015 by Totally Bound Publishing, Newland House, The Point, Weaver Road, Lincoln, LN6 3QN, United Kingdom.

Totally Bound Publishing is a subsidiary of Totally Entwined Group Limited.

PURRFECT PROTECTOR

Dedication

To Faith, thank you.

For the real Kale

Chapter One

"I really don't see why we need to be here, Caleb. Every model in the limelight gets crazy mail. It's nothing new." Kale rubbed his left temple as he felt a migraine coming on. He didn't want to be there in the first place, but his manager had insisted. Sometimes having his brother as his boss sucked.

"You're right. Everyone in the business I've talked to says the same thing"—his brother held up a hand before Kale could do so much as open his mouth—"but none of *them* received an eyeball in a box hand-delivered to a closed set they were working on."

Kale didn't have a response. He was saved from trying to find one when the secretary behind the reception desk of Shifter Protection Specialists, Inc. touched her headset when it beeped then waved them forward. "Mr. McCade will see you now."

"Come on."

Kale had no option but to follow his brother into the large office.

As he entered the room, it surprised him that Mr. McCade was his height and looked nothing like the picture he'd built up in his mind of a bodyguard. The company was supposed to be the best, and people in the personal protection industry whispered about it. He might not agree that he needed their protection but that didn't mean he hadn't done his homework before coming here.

"Welcome, Mr. and Mr. Andrews. I'm Scott McCade. I understand that you have a need for our services." The man stood and walked to them, then he shook their hands before gesturing for Kale and Caleb to take a seat.

"Thank you, Mr. McCade. Recently my brother has received some disturbing letters and last week something that quite frankly scared me. He got an eyeball in a hand-delivered package to a photo shoot that only seven or so people knew about. I've talked with all of them and each one claims not to have told anyone—and I believe them."

Scott McCade didn't give away any of his thoughts, but Kale got the feeling the man was surprised.

"I see," Scott said, without anything in his voice to reveal what he thought about it. "I read the copy of the report you sent me and I see you do have a problem we can help with. With cases like this one, there are certain indicators we look for. Buzz words and the like that suggest the writer of threatening mail will escalate to violent behavior. The letters you shared with me are full of them. I recommend a close protection guard be with you at all times until we can root out the person who sent them."

Kale sighed and looked at the ceiling. He didn't need to hear another lecture about his safety. "I'm the flavor of the month on the fashion scene right now. That is bound to attract the crazies…"

Mr. McCade nodded. "Of course. So you know other models who have received animal body parts in the mail?"

Kale stopped short. "Well…no. But…that was a *real* eyeball? I thought it was a prop." He shook off the tendrils of fear growing in his gut. He'd worked too hard and kissed too many asses to be where he was—at the top of his game. There were so many influential designers clamoring for a piece of him—wanting him to do campaigns, runways and television adverts—that he had his pick of bids. *Nothing* was going to jeopardize that. He was twenty-five and he figured he had a three-year window in this industry before he had to switch to runway-only jobs.

It was a fickle industry but Kale loved what he did for a living.

"It doesn't matter. Whoever it was will get bored and find someone else to focus on," Kale insisted.

Mr. McCade raised an eyebrow but said nothing more. Kale was used to being treated as an airhead and, if he were honest, he understood why his brother was insisting on hiring a bodyguard. However, Kale needed to keep the three big jobs he had lined up—the fashion shoot in Paris, the runway in Milan and the group shoot in New York. If he made those three events his best work, then he would be set for offers for his full three-year plan and have contacts to make a career in fashion after that.

"Well, Mr. Andrews, it appears there is nothing we can do for you." Scott McCade clasped his hands together and leaned back in his chair.

"Thank—"

Mr. McCade cut him off with a wave of his hand. "I was talking to your brother. He seems to be the one with the sense."

Shocked, Kale sat back. What had he done to deserve such a dismissal?

"Please. Despite what my brother thinks, this is serious. It started with a few letters every month or so, then every week to every day, and now he's getting packages like this with cards saying '*I'll be watching over you, my love*'. This is *escalating* and I don't want to wait around to see what comes next. The hotel security where my brother lives had a breach yesterday when an unidentified male managed to gain access to Kale's floor. I can't always be with him when he's on a campaign or at an event, and I don't think I'm much protection when I am. I need your company's help."

Kale shot a sideways glance at Caleb. His brother was putting it on a bit thick. Sure, he had a fan who was more than a little creepy, but that was it. His hotel housed some very famous people — far more famous than him — and they didn't take security lightly.

Caleb tightened his jaw and the vein on this brother's forehead pulsed. His brother *was* really scared about this.

Mr. McCade sat forward again and placed his hands on the stack of letters Kale guessed were addressed to him or Caleb. "I can offer several protection options, but unless your brother agrees, there is nothing we can do to protect him."

"I agree," Kale said quietly. If he'd thought all this had really bothered Caleb so much, he wouldn't have been so difficult.

Scott McCade looked at him with a strange expression, and Kale had the feeling that he had risen in the man's estimation.

"Very well, then. I agree with your brother, Mr. Andrews. You need protection, but I also get the feeling that you aren't going to be an easy protectee. You are gay, correct?"

Instantly on guard, Kale sat back and narrowed his gaze. "Yes."

"Good. That will make it easier to explain the presence of the man I'm assigning to protect you. He'll be your lover."

"My lover?"

"Yes. To explain why he'll be on set with you, you can tell everyone who asks that he's the jealous sort or that he loves watching you work," Mr. McCade clarified in a tone that suggested he was already making plans and Kale's agreement had merely been a formality.

Kale's thoughts were confirmed when the man picked up the phone handset and asked the secretary to call in someone called Aleksi. Mr. McCade turned his attention back to them with a slight smile that Kale didn't trust.

"Aleksi will join us in a few minutes. I hope you don't have a problem with cats."

* * * *

The last thing Aleksi wanted to do was to babysit another party boy who thought his looks gave him the privilege to treat people like dirt. Then the party boys seemed surprised when some of those people wanted revenge.

His last high-priority job had gone a little off course and had resulted in him spending a few nights in a Russian holding facility, but it hadn't been his fault. His protectee hadn't been honest with them and it turned out he was actually a prince from Dubai on the run from a terrorist group wanting to use him as a political prisoner. To say the team sent to kidnap the prince was met with a less than friendly welcome was an understatement. Then the Russian secret police had gotten involved, weapons had been drawn, bombs had gone off and one thing had led to another.

Hence, the time in the holding facility where his hosts had taken turns trying to learn his name and the location of the prince. Aleksi grinned at the memory. He'd made two of the interrogators cry. *Fun times.*

The terms of his protection detail had been met and the prince had arrived unmolested, at the top-secret meeting to discuss peace treaties with the United Kingdom and the United States then had traveled home safely with a colleague of Aleksi's.

Despite everything working out fine, Scott still had his panties in a knot. Something to do with Aleksi not taking care of himself and scaring his friends. *Rubbish!* Scott knew he'd be okay. After all, they'd been trained by the same man—Scott's brother, Robert.

But since then, all his assignments had been babysitting for stuck-up pretty boys who drove him crazy. If this was another one of those assignments, he'd pay back the company fee and eat the protectee himself.

After reading the text summoning him to Scott's office to meet his new bestie, Aleksi shoved his phone back into his pocket. He walked to the door, looking over his shoulder at the mountain of plush cushions he'd been sent by the prince as a thank you. "I'll be back soon." His inner cat was practically climbing the walls in frustration. He hadn't even gotten to stretch out and sleep on any of the pretty pillows yet.

Sighing, he left his office and locked the door behind him. His fellow bodyguards and protectors were like his brothers, but one or two of them would jump at the chance to make off with his cushions if they could. *Sneaky bastards.*

He jogged down the hall and opened Scott's door without knocking. The scents of the two new humans in the room hit him and his cat froze. The two men looked similar but the one wearing the plain shirt and jeans was a bit shinier. That was the only way to describe him. Shiny.

"Aleksi," Scott greeted.

"This better be good, Scott. I had a date with soft and silky."

The two humans turned around to look at him, their eyes widening. Aleksi wasn't offended. This happened a lot. He was six foot ten and, because of his animal's nature, he carried a lot of muscle.

Shiny tilted up his head in surprise. Aleksi caught the flash of annoyance and disgust, even as he scented the male's arousal. This might turn out to be more interesting than he'd first thought.

Kale almost swallowed his tongue as the man Scott had called for entered the room. The newcomer's shoulders touched each side of the doorframe and—if he wasn't mistaken—the guy also had to bend his knees a little to avoid hitting his head on the top.

Wow. He didn't know who Soft and Silky was but he'd be willing to throw down if he got to keep the man who had just entered the office as the prize.

Kale had always had a thing for muscles and this Aleksi was built like a Thor action figure, complete with golden locks. This was the man who was going to pretend to be his lover? *Why was I reluctant to do this again?*

"Because you're an idiot," Caleb whispered next to him before elbowing him in the ribs.

Shit, he must have said that aloud.

"Hey, watch it. You know makeup doesn't cover bruises well."

"Then stop embarrassing me." His brother fussed with his tie and apologized to the two other men in the office.

Kale glared. Caleb was so stuffy. "I haven't done anything!"

"Actually, you *were* talking out loud." Scott McCade looked amused.

Aleksi was inspecting Kale as if he were an interesting insect.

"As you may have guessed," Scott continued, "this is Aleksi, and he will be your close protection guard until we uncover who is behind the letters and packages. Aleksi, this is Kale Andrews, a model who has a fan sending him letters and apparently an animal eyeball."

Aleksi turned back to Scott. Kale breathed a sigh of relief. As hot as the man was, he didn't like being the main target of that assessing gaze. There was something powerful and dangerous lurking underneath that beautiful surface.

"Human?"

"No, animal, but delivered to a closed set with limited staff's knowledge."

They were actually talking about it as if it was an everyday occurrence. Despite his earlier argument that other people had had weird things sent to them in the past, the body part in the mail had seriously wigged him out. He was just glad he hadn't opened the thing himself.

His phone buzzed and Kale ignored the accusing look his brother sent him. Kale flipped open the leather case to read the message anyway. "Damn, the designer for the new Armani campaign pulled out last minute. Philippe needs me at the shoot within the hour."

Caleb frowned at him and Kale knew he was winding up for a lecture. He didn't know what it was between Philippe and his brother but the two men hated each other. "Can't he call in one of his bunnies? And why isn't he calling *me*? I'm your agent."

"Probably because he knows you'll say no. You know none of his *bunnies*, as you put it, meet the brief. He wants the dark hair, blue eyes, not too slim but not too built, classic look. I meet the criteria without being feminine. His bunnies don't." His phone buzzed again. "He says if I can't come then he loses a whole day as he searches for a new model. I know you don't like him but c'mon... He could lose his job."

His brother dragged a hand through his hair and groaned in frustration. "Fine. Go, but take your bodyguard with you. Perhaps it will stop Philippe from groping you."

Kale bit the inside of his cheek to stop himself from smiling. Little did his brother know that Philippe only flirted and pawed at him when Caleb was there. When he wasn't, the man treated Kale with nothing but friendly respect.

Instead of saying anything more to Caleb, Kale turned back to Aleksi. He tried to give the man his signature come-hither smile, but his heart was pumping too fast for that look and he know it came across as shy. He was never shy. He posed for photos that people saw all over the world, sometimes in less than a Speedo. He could snap his fingers and have at least a dozen gorgeous men kneeling at his feet, begging him to sleep with them. Kale Andrews was *not* shy.

"Come on then, pretty. Let's get this over with," Aleksi said with a sigh, seemingly completely unimpressed.

Chapter Two

Aleksi knew he'd pissed off the pretty man but the comment the man's brother had made about this Philippe designer pawing at Kale made his cat hiss. No matter how many times he told himself this was simply going to be another job, the same as any other, he couldn't seem to believe it.

Kale was fascinating. While Scott and Caleb Andrews had signed the protection contracts, Aleksi had watched the man he was going to protect. As the man himself had described, Kale had a classically handsome look with his dark hair and bright blue eyes. Usually Aleksi went for men much bigger, almost as big as himself, because he was afraid he'd break anyone too small. There was something about Kale, though, that drew him. The ten-and-a-half-inch height difference between made an interesting change.

As they drove to the photo shoot, Aleksi decided to figure out how the male model felt about shifters. "Is there a reason you were reluctant to have protection from Shifter Protection Specialists, Inc.?"

Kale, to his credit, picked up on the question Aleksi hadn't asked straight away.

"I don't have anything against shifters. I didn't want all this fuss. It's just a few letters."

"And an eyeball," he added. It concerned him that the human seemed so calm about it all.

The man went a little green "Yes, thank you. I haven't forgotten."

"Good, you shouldn't."

They pulled into the studio parking structure. Aleksi smiled when Kale huffed and sighed as Aleksi made the man stay in the car until he had scoped the surroundings, checking for any threats.

He noted all the cars around them, looking for anything that stood out. Other than a van taking up two spaces and a Mini Cooper with a small stuffed toy hanging from the tailpipe, nothing seemed out of place in the environment. Aleksi drew in a deep breath. He scented no one close by.

"All clear." He banged on the roof of the vehicle.

When Kale stepped out of the car and immediately headed for the elevator without so much as a look, Aleksi smiled again. The model could act unaffected, but Aleksi's nose could tell that Kale had enjoyed watching him do the security sweep. The human kept looking at his biceps too.

"Remember, it's best that you introduce me as your boyfriend," Aleksi reiterated.

"I don't understand why I can't say you're my bodyguard."

"Because then the behavior of whoever is sending you letters may escalate dangerously. We want to catch him, not push him into doing something stupid." He set a fast pace. There were too many places someone could hide.

Before they entered the elevator, Aleksi peered in first then guided Kale inside while looking back to make sure no one was trying to ambush them from behind. He still didn't scent anyone on this level of the parking structure, but there were certain agents on the market who could disguise a person's scent.

"Something stupid?"

Aleksi shrugged. "Some fans become stalkers. Others become criminals and a few have hurt the object of their obsession when they weren't able to make them do what they imagined."

As much as he didn't want to scare his protectee, he understood that Kale needed to know this was serious and not something to be shrugged off because it didn't fit into his lifestyle.

"I'm not sure I wanted to know that," Kale commented with a grimace.

"You need to be aware of the danger. If you're right and this is merely a fan who got carried away and will move on, then I'm sure all this will be cleared up in the next day or two. If I'm right and this is a credible threat, then one way or the other this will end soon."

A tense silence followed and he started to feel guilty about his honesty. Perhaps his attraction to the model was throwing him off his game.

"That's okay. I meant what I said at the office. I'll do what you tell me when it concerns my safety. I keep my word." Kale stabbed the studio floor button angrily and went quiet.

Aleksi was about to say something when the ding of the elevator doors sounded and, just like that, Kale seemed to shake off the attitude. It was the same way a fighter put on his game face before combat.

"By the way, Mr. McCade insinuated that you were a cat. What kind of cat?"

Grinning, Aleksi ignored Kale's gaze and kept looking through the decreasing gap as the elevator doors slid closed. "I'm a saber-tooth tiger."

* * * *

Kale was certain this shoot was going to be his last because he was going to murder the Frenchman. Philippe had wanted him to wear the suits and after an hour or so, that campaign photo list was complete. Somehow, the smooth-talking man managed to convince him to do some test shots for the new fragrance campaign. Kale didn't mind—it was a great opportunity—but all he could think about was his new hot shifter shadow. The man was distractingly handsome and with Kale wearing a scrap of nude fabric that was somehow supposed to preserve his modesty, that was a problem—a big problem. Kale exited the changing area.

Aleksi was still in the same place as when Kale had gone to change. His bodyguard stood leaning against the wall, looking bored and completely disinterested with the whole fashion-shoot thing. Kale guessed the shifter must be wondering what he'd gotten himself into. No doubt Aleksi was used to protecting important people in high-adrenaline situations.

Kale was still reeling from the revelation that this god of a man was a freaking saber-tooth tiger. The shifter in question must have felt Kale's gaze on him, because the man looked his way, and Kale swore he saw a flash of the dangerous cat within him. That should have scared Kale, but it only made the blood race in his veins and he couldn't get enough air. He took a step forward.

Philippe chose that moment to notice he'd come out of the dressing room—and by room, Kale meant a small area marked off with standing Japanese blinds.

"Ah, good. You're ready. I don't want makeup for you on this one, so you'll be fine with just the minimum you're still wearing from the suit set."

Kale let the designer lead him away until he stood in the middle of the set Philippe had finished arranging. Unlike the previous white scenery, where he knew the computer guys would imagine some fantastical background, this one was all of black and gray. It also held a heavy velvet-and-silk curtain and a black-red chaise with the old-fashioned filigree carving on the wood. It was a dark mix of vintage and sexy.

"Now, you've seen the last few campaigns and they're a bit samey," Philippe drawled with a dismissive wave of his hand.

The enthusiastic designer leaned in close to him. Kale couldn't say why, but he shot a quick glance over at Aleksi to see the man looking elsewhere. Something told him the shifter was fully aware of what was going on all around the room, though, and he pulled away so he wasn't as close to Philippe. Aleksi was supposed to be his lover and he didn't want to disrespect the shifter, even if it was only a cover story.

"My higher-ups have given me the nod to run with an idea that's a little out there," Philippe continued.

Kale glanced back and dropped his easygoing tone. "*How* out there?" In this *outfit*, that could mean anything. Philippe was aware of Kale's limits, knew he wouldn't do full frontal nudity and that Kale also wouldn't grope women for the sake of 'art'.

It had been a problem at the beginning of his career, but Kale had made the promise to himself when he'd decided to be a model that he needed to draw some lines and not cross them—professionally and personally.

Philippe smirked. "Don't worry. I remember your aversion to the fairer sex."

"I don't have an *aversion* to women. I just don't want to make out with them," Kale corrected sardonically.

"I don't blame you, *cher*. But no, that is not what I want you to do. I want you stretched out and draped in fabric, doing your best smoldering looks."

"Okay, but how is that different from a hundred other campaigns? No offense."

"Because you'll be doing it with Liam." Almost the instant Philippe said the name, another male model appeared beside the Frenchman, wearing the exact same thing as Kale, including heavy black eye makeup with his blond hair slicked back as if he'd recently gotten out of the shower.

"Hi," Liam greeted with a cocky smile. He sidled up to Kale before wrapping an arm tightly around his waist.

"Hello," he replied with a forced smile, extracting himself from the man's hold. Kale shot Philippe a dark look. The man knew better than not to warn him about a grabber. The designer had the decency to appear chided...for all of a minute. Then the man fell back into his over-the-top designer persona and sashayed off to talk to the photographer about the lighting.

Some days the modeling gig is just a big headache.

Liam moved over to the chaise and Kale followed, but instead of sprawling over the thing, Kale went to the larger side and perched on the arm. He thought this would be fine to start with until he gauged how far Philippe intended to go with this idea. Liam evidently had other plans, as the man pulled him down onto the seat and painfully gripped the top of his arm to stop him from moving away.

"Listen to me. You may be some fuck-toy star at the moment, but *I'm* the next big thing and you are not going to ruin this for me by being a fucking prude."

The viciously hissed words surprised Kale. On the few male-only shoots he'd done—usually high-end menswear—the models had been arrogant and self-obsessed but few of them had been openly hostile.

"Well as the *star*, as you put it, I'll give you a little advice. Don't be such a prick. You're not good-looking enough to offset that much ugliness." Kale spat the words back at the other model, putting on his best bitch voice. It was the only way to get through to these types. This was another reason for his three-year plan. He wouldn't be able to put up with all the falseness and keep up the front for much longer. He wanted to create, to be part of the process that put all the pieces together for campaigns and he wanted to do it for a good cause instead of another in a long line of celebrity fragrances.

A quick look reassured him that Philippe was still talking with the photographer. It wouldn't do for his employer to see this. Kale took hold of the model's wrist and applied pressure to the joint.

The maneuver was one of the few things he remembered from the self-defense classes his brother used to teach. If a person squeezed enough and in exactly the right place, the tendons in the fingers loosened.

There.

Liam's hand opened and Kale moved out of his reach and let go. "Do *not* grab me like that again. Or this will be the last job you ever get."

Kale wasn't important enough to influence the industry big shots but Liam didn't know that. His threat worked. Liam backed down, but Kale recognized the anger in the man's eyes.

People like Liam didn't appreciate being put in their place.

"Now, boys. I want romance and raw desire. Real emotion. Kale, I know you're always good. Liam, try not to ruin it." Philippe's voice came just before the lights brightened and the wind machine in the corner turned on to move the set's billowy fabric gently.

Liam tensed at Philippe's words and disguised an eye roll by pushing a stray hair back from his face.

This is going to be a long shoot. Kale sighed.

Aleksi had to stop himself from going over to the set and ripping the other model away from Kale. He clawed his fingers into the wall behind him. Ever since the annoying designer had gotten that glint in his eye, things had started going south. The clean-cut suits were gone and Kale had emerged from behind the blind in only a skimpy little piece of material that left almost nothing to the imagination.

What made it worse was that Aleksi had scented the man's discomfort. He'd seen Kale take a step toward him before the damn Frenchman had whisked him and the slut away.

With his heightened tiger senses, Aleksi could smell the new model too well for his comfort. There were at least four other scents, both male and female, on the man that were far too strong to be anything other than sex. He also detected the acrid stench of drugs— methamphetamine, if he wasn't mistaken. He'd spent a few years as a consultant for the DEA. Liam was good at covering the signs. Aleksi would give the man that. No puffy eyes or nose and only the tiniest of body tremors that Aleksi noticed only because he was looking for them.

In the five minutes or so he'd been watching the man, the other more subtle behavioral signs were there—agitation, aggression, deluded sense of power, mood swings and paranoia.

When the two nearly naked models had been on opposite ends of the chaise he couldn't decide was tacky or not, he'd watched the process with fascination. From where Aleksi stood, he could view the final shots loading on the monitor beside Philippe. It was surprising how the most subtle and miniscule of changes in expression and body placement changed the final effect of a photograph. Then the photographer directed Kale and Liam to lie on the seat together and things started getting even more uncomfortable.

"I want you to get closer. You need to look like nothing else exists in the world but each other. That's great, Kale. Liam, move your hand away from his face. I can't see Kale properly in the shot. Now you're blocking him with your shoulder. Liam!"

Aleksi growled when Liam let his hand linger too long on Kale's throat, leaving red marks. In four long strides, Aleksi closed the distance between him and the struggling models. He got there not a second too late. Kale tried to sit up and the Liam blocked his escape and grabbed for Kale's throat again.

Quick as the cat he was, he shot out his hand and captured Liam's wrist. The model was too stupid to know when he was outmatched and he tried to claw at Kale's beautiful skin instead. All of Aleksi's patience evaporated. He let his eyes shift and a deep growl rumbled through his chest. No one could mistake the threat of a superior predator.

He heard a gasp and glanced away from Liam to see that Kale was okay. His protectee stared up at him, mouth agape, gaze fixed on Aleksi's eyes.

From the size of Liam's pupils, he was too drugged up to realize what was happening and still fought Aleksi's grip. Aleksi glanced at his charge and dragged Liam off Kale and then the seat. He resisted the urge to throw Liam. Instead, he simply shoved the male back a few steps. "Leave."

The one growled word seemed to set the model off again and Liam tensed as if to attack Aleksi. However, Philippe got in between them first. Aleksi was a little disappointed. His cat wanted to play and beating the drugged man would be a good game for them, as a house cat with a mouse, batting Liam about and chasing him when he tried to run away.

"You heard him. Leave my studio. *Now*. You nearly marked up his face. You'll be lucky to work in this industry again."

As Philippe spoke, Aleksi flicked his gaze past the designer and saw the photographer talking quietly into a phone.

"He's *nothing*!" Liam shouted. "I should be the star, the golden boy. Me!"

Aleksi kept himself between Liam and Kale, tracking the irate man's erratic gestures and movement. There wasn't anywhere Liam could hide a weapon in that getup but Aleksi had learned addicts could be unpredictable.

The door to the studio opened and two relatively large security men came in, then they dragged Liam out, kicking and screaming. Once the threat was clear of the studio and Aleksi could no longer hear the man's crazed yelling, he turned to face Kale, inspecting him.

His charge still looked uninjured, apart from the red marks on his neck that stood out against his lightly golden skin. Another soft growl escaped him. Liam never should have touched Kale.

"Are you okay?" Aleksi asked.

Kale nodded slowly, his eyes wide and body stiff as he rose from the chaise. Aleksi realized the problem, stopped growling and forced his eyes to change back from cat to human.

"Sorry," he said, even though he wasn't sure what he was apologizing for. Aleksi coughed, covering the final growl of discontent from his cat. After this assignment, he would really need to go to his safe house away from the city and run for a few days as his animal.

Kale rubbed the marks on his throat and shook his head, shooting another look toward the door. "None of this was your fault."

"I thought I'd scared you." It happened often around his protectees, but it had never bothered him much before. *Why is Kale different?*

Kale tensed then surprised Aleksi by smiling. "Nah...I like cats."

Aleksi grinned as his cat took notice of the model for a different reason than Kale being nearly naked. Kale was just different enough to be interesting and make him curious. Cats loved things that made them curious.

Chapter Three

Philippe had been full of apologies for the episode with Liam and had begged Kale to do a *couple more shots*. The couple more shots quickly turned into another hour or so on set in that scrap of fabric, sprawled over the chaise in a series of poses that had Aleksi hiding in the shadows of the studio so he didn't embarrass himself.

Growing so hard he was certain he was testing the tensile strength of his black denim jeans wasn't exactly in the close-protection-specialist handbook, but watching Kale's taught body, slightly oiled with strategically placed black and gray body powders to enhance his muscles and the bone structure, was severely challenging his control. He had the distinct feeling that Kale knew it too. The smoldering looks sent his way for a good portion of the shots had to be more than a coincidence.

What made it worse was that those expressions were accompanied with an arched back, as if he was in ecstasy — or a bowed body, experiencing a lover's touch, or even a hand reaching out for a lost love.

Geez, listen to me. I'm waxing lyrical about my protectee. He needed to hit something before he had to hand in his man card. If his brothers could hear him now, they'd have ammunition against him for years.

The designer went wild at those expressions and Aleksi could scent not only Kale's slight arousal but Philippe's and the photographer's as well. His cat was becoming agitated and he finally breathed a deep sighed of relief when Kale called an end to it all.

Kale quickly skipped off to change and they left not long after with Kale promising to call Philippe to organize a double date with them and one of his latest boy toys. For a moment, Kale faltered, but Aleksi stepped in, laughing and promising they'd make an evening of it.

Aleksi steered Kale out of the studio, his arm around the model's waist, because he felt Philippe's speculative gaze on them. "Where to now?"

"Uh...home, I guess. Wait—are you staying there too?"

Smiling at the shock in the model's voice, Aleksi simply nodded and scanned the elevator area. "Yes, I'll ask Scott to swing by my place later and pick up my bag."

Out the corner of his eye, he saw Kale frown. "You have a bag already packed?"

"Yes, it's SOP—standard operating procedure. The only reason I didn't have the bag ready to go in my office was because I was supposed to be on a break for another few days."

As they exited the elevator, something tickled Aleksi's senses. He pulled Kale close to his back and shushed the man when Kale opened his mouth. He couldn't smell anyone or hear anything other than engines and the normal noise level of a parking structure.

Something was pulling at him, though.

"Stick close to my back. We're getting to the car as quickly as possible," Aleksi warned, waiting just long enough to feel Kale nod against him before setting a fast pace. There were more cars than when they'd arrived hours ago and more people walking around too, going to and from their vehicles. Nothing out of the ordinary or anything dangerous stood out, but his cat was on edge, as if they were being watched.

They quickly reached the car and Aleksi made sure Kale stayed with him as he circled it to check for any devices or signs of tampering. He reached into his pocket and pulled out the small mirror he always carried then leaned over to stick it on the toe of his boot so he could see the undercarriage. It was good practice in his line of work to do this after every time a vehicle was left unsupervised.

"Isn't that overkill?"

"Anyone motivated enough can look on the Internet and learn how to make an IED. It's better to be over prepared than caught unawares," he explained as he completed checking the car.

"I could have lived a happy life without knowing that," Kale drawled.

Aleksi chuckled and opened the door to the backseat. It would give him greater maneuverability if he had to implement offensive driving techniques. "In you get."

"Thank you, Alfred," Kale said, his tone snotty.

"I'm not calling you Batman — or sir."

He couldn't remember a protection detail being this much fun before.

Kale was quiet for several minutes as Aleksi started the car. He glanced at his protectee in the rearview mirror. "Hey, I will if you want me to."

Kale looked up and met his gaze.

After shutting off the engine, Aleksi spun in his seat. "What is it?"

"I think someone was in the car while we were in the studio," Kale said shakily.

Aleksi noticed a small package wedged under the seat next to Kale. The way the seat curved stylishly had hidden it from view when he'd checked through the windows before Kale had entered. Aleksi filed that information away to account for the blind spot next time. It pissed him off that he'd missed it.

He didn't wait before climbing into the backseat. He pressed Kale up against the locked door, shielding the man with his body while he visually inspected the package.

There were no scents on the box. It must have been sprayed with an anti-shifter-detection compound. To work this well and not have any trace on it was odd. Only the very best military-grade stuff was that effective and it was not easy to come by — or cheap. Owing to the expense, the military rarely only used ones like it. The chemicals in them also had a tendency to damage the user's respiratory and nervous systems.

"I'm going to open the package, okay?"

"Yes."

Aleksi fingered the purple ribbon tying the eighteen-by-five-inch box, looking for any kind of trigger, and quickly undid it when he found none. He'd usually make his protectee wait outside in a safe area but he still had that tingly feeling at the back of his neck that said someone was watching them.

Touching the box as little as possible, he gingerly peeled back the paper. The police might be able to pull some prints off it. Aleksi opened the box to reveal a single purple rose — or what used to be a rose. All the flower petals had been ripped off, crumpled up and thrown to the bottom of the box.

"At least it wasn't another animal part," Kale pointed out, as Aleksi let him peer over his shoulder.

He spotted a white piece of parchment underneath the prickly stem and picked it up. "Hang on, there's a note with it.

Be a good boy. Good boys get pretty flowers. I'm coming for you, my love.

"Well, that's…creepy."

"Yes," Aleksi agreed. Kale might not realize just how right he was. Whoever was doing this had connections and money to get his hands on the anti-shifter detection spray. They would also have to have eyes on Kale to know about the last-minute appointment with Philippe at the studio.

Aleksi had a hunch how the man was doing it, but he didn't have any proof. Without evidence, the police assigned to the case would have their hands tied, especially as they didn't have a suspect. "Give me your phone."

"Why?" Kale handed him his cell.

At least Kale wasn't fighting Aleksi in protecting him anymore.

"I'm going to play a hunch," he told Kale.

He handed his phone to Kale in exchange and instructed him to press Speed Dial Two. "Tell Scott to have the police officers handling your case at your hotel in plain clothes in an hour. Tell him to call your brother and instruct him to ignore all texts from your phone until told otherwise." He waited for Kale to do as he'd said before he shot off a text on Kale's phone to the man's brother.

On way back to room. Ditched new bf. Feeling tired. Call you later.

A quick scroll through Kale's message streams had let him know the man only shortened long words to text speak, so he had matched the style. Now all they had to do was drive to the hotel and see if his hunch was right. Aleksi hoped it wasn't, though.

Kale ended the call and watched silently as Aleksi squeezed his large frame back through the gap and into the driver's seat. The shifter had scared him in the studio when Liam had snapped, throwing the jerk off him as if he'd weighed nothing. Then scared him again when the shifter had made him stick to his back as they'd checked the car for bombs. Everything was beginning to feel a little too real. He was a model, for fuck's sake! Bombs had nothing to do with his life.

"So, what now?"

"Now we head back to your room at the hotel."

Kale looked daggers at the driver's seat. "That's it? That's all you're going to give me."

"Yep." He didn't have to see his face to know the damn shifter was smiling. The man had been doing it all day, as if Kale were some new, fascinating pet that might do something interesting at any moment.

"Tell me," Kale insisted.

"No."

A small part of him hated that he had only this card left to play. It seemed like cheating. But the shifter had brought it on himself. "You work for me and I demand you tell me what the hell is going on."

"Actually, *Mr. Andrews*, I work for Shifter Protection Specialists, Inc. and we are being contracted by your brother to protect you. So whichever way you spin it, I don't have to answer you. Good try, though." Aleksi started the engine and reversed out of the space before proceeding to drive away.

Kale had never been so riled by someone before. The smugness in the shifter's voice was infuriating. "Perhaps we can stop at the store on the way and get you some kitty toys so you don't scratch the furniture."

"Come on now. You can do better than that. Besides, I think I've found a *kitty toy* already," the shifter shot back as they drove out of the parking structure.

Again, Kale didn't have to look to know Aleksi was laughing at him. His face burned with embarrassment. He refused to acknowledge that he enjoyed arguing with Aleksi. "Just shut up and drive."

* * * *

The ride passed in silence and so did the trip up to his room in the elevator. Together, they walked toward his door. Kale hadn't spotted anyone suspicious, nor had the police officers he knew were dealing with the official complaint Caleb had made him file.

"Stay close," Aleksi hissed quietly, as they turned the corner and his door came into view.

Kale jumped but stepped closer to Aleksi. He couldn't see anything or anyone dangerous. There was only Barry from housekeeping. The guy was nice and a really good artist from the sketches Kale had seen one day, but he hadn't been as talkative lately. Perhaps Kale should see if he'd said anything to offend the man and apologize.

Barry turned their way and Kale waved.

He shot a surprised look at the shifter when Aleksi wound an arm around his waist and dragged him close, snaking his hand into Kale's back pocket as they walked. "Stay very close."

Kale refused to think about why being this close to Aleksi and having the man's hand on his ass made his heart beat a little out of sync. He'd never been this attracted and simultaneously annoyed by someone. "It's just Barry. I've known him the entire time I've lived here."

Aleksi nodded but kept his attention focused on Barry and the housekeeping cart. They kept walking and Kale let the shifter increase the pace as they passed Barry and came within a few feet of Kale's door. Aleksi took the key in his hand, quickly opened the door and ushered Kale inside.

Kale almost jumped out of his skin when the shifter didn't turn on a light and instead hid beside the doorway, motioning for Kale to step further into the room then stop and turn away. Kale was only a foot or two from the door. Something in his mind told him to act naturally. Whatever was going on, he guessed Aleksi didn't want him to blow the deception.

"G-grab me a beer too, would you? Bottle opener is in the second draw, babe." He tried to sound normal, as if he was talking to his lover and Aleksi was really headed to the kitchen.

Barely two breaths later, Kale heard light footsteps coming his way. He tried pretending he didn't hear them by fiddling with his coat, as if he were having trouble with one of the buttons.

"Have you been a good boy? I've kept my *eye* on you."

The whispered words in his ear made his blood run cold. He jumped away. The second he moved, he felt the disturbance of the air behind him. Barry must have tried to grab him.

Kale stumbled over his feet as he spun around and backed away from the man he'd called his friend. He went down hard, his ass aching from the impact. "Barry!"

"Good boys are more careful. You're coming with me now," Barry said, eyes wild and wide. The man fully stepped into the room and reached for him. Kale scrambled back until he hit the heavy white leather sofa. It must have been obvious, because Barry grinned, showing all his teeth like some sort of hysterical hyena, and grabbed for him again.

Barry never got close enough to touch him, though. Aleksi had been so still and quiet that Kale had forgotten about the shifter. He didn't have time even to cringe as the shifter jumped into action. Aleksi pounced on Barry and, despite Barry's struggles and yells, Aleksi had the man flat on his stomach, legs spread and hands held behind his back.

A completely inappropriate thought about him came to mind. Kale would be in Barry's position with Aleksi on top of him like that—for completely different reasons, of course. The little jolt of excitement shot straight to his groin and made him half-hard.

The worst thing was that Aleksi snapped his head around to stare at Kale, eyes pure cat and all knowing—and the look really shouldn't have made Kale as hot as it did.

The sound of people running toward them caught Kale's attention. Two police officers entered the room as planned.

"What's going on here?"

The demand was made by a slightly overweight cop in street clothes. Crumbs clung to his shirt and sweat beaded his brow as if he'd run a marathon instead of the length of the hall. The other officer looked as though she couldn't stand her partner. The male officer repeated his question and pulled his weapon.

Aleksi growled when the officer pointed the gun in Kale's direction. The officer quickly changed his target, watching Aleksi closely. No doubt taking in the sight of Aleksi's bright cat eyes.

"Officer David, you know why we're here. Mr. McCade called us to set this up. His operative has obviously caught the culprit who sent the stalker mail to Mr. Andrews."

Officer David ignored his partner for the most part, still keeping the gun trained on Aleksi. "How do we know that? This *shifter* may have just attacked this man," the officer snarled. It was clear from the way he hesitated before saying shifter that it wasn't the word the officer really wanted to use. Shifters didn't take well to being insulted by derogatory words about their nature. The cop probably looked on shifters as animals or monsters.

Kale slowly got to his feet, not wanting to startle either of the officers, and stepped toward the female cop. "I'm the one who filed the report about letters and packages and the man you're pointing the gun at is my bodyguard. The guy on the ground is Barry, part of the hotel's housekeeping staff."

Barry took the opportunity to start yelling. "The shifter attacked me. I was trying to help Mr. Andrews and this animal tackled me to the floor and tried to eat me!" As if to sell the lie, Barry wailed pitifully and started sobbing.

It was obvious the cries were fake, but it gave Officer David the excuse he needed to stick to his prejudices and steady the gun on Aleksi, who was silent and still…waiting.

"Officer Dav—" the female officer began.

Officer David was having none of it. Kale had seen that look before from his father. A man like that had such hatred for anyone and anything different, that once there was an excuse for him to let it out, there was no dissuading him from it.

Pandering to it was the only option in order to minimize the damage.

Gently placing himself next to Officer David, Kale tried to shake off the nervousness and pasted a relieved and grateful smile on his face. "Thank you for responding so quickly. I was so scared."

When he saw Officer David's gaze linger on him, Kale realized he still wore some makeup from the photo shoot. He ducked his head shyly and let his hair fall to frame his face and eyes as he looked up through his lashes at the officer.

"I…well…you're welcome. Now I need you to stand aside while I deal with the other two," Officer David sputtered, puffing out his chest like some sort of male bird presenting for a prospective female mate.

It nauseated Kale.

He flicked his gaze to the female cop. She watched him with a mixture of interest and disgust. Disgust at what, Kale didn't know, but it was clear he wouldn't be able to count on her for any back up.

"I don't want to get in the way. I just worry Barry might try to hurt me if the *shifter* moves." He was laying it on a bit thick and part of him recoiled at the emphasis he placed on the word shifter. But by speaking in the same way Officer David had, it would create the appearance of like-mindedness. His college class in psychology came in useful at times.

Latching onto Kale's common use of shifter, Officer David relaxed and slowly started lowering his weapon, staring at Kale instead of Aleksi and Barry.

"That's all right. Officer Hadley, cuff the suspect while I protect the victim."

Officer Hadley, the female officer, stepped forward and produced a set of handcuffs from her belt before approaching Aleksi and Barry without a word. She left Kale to contend with Officer David, who was standing a little too close and touching him too much for Kale's liking.

Officer David crept his hand from where he had rested it on Kale's shoulder to down Kale's back to cup his ass. "Don't worry. I'll protect you."

Kale almost gagged.

Officer Hadley instructed Aleksi to get off Barry and the shifter did so without comment or complaint, looking for all the world like butter wouldn't melt in his mouth. But it was too late for calm innocence. Both officers were wary of the enormous shifter. Kale would bet that one wrong move might get Aleksi shot.

"Step over to the wall." Officer Hadley was careful to keep out of Aleksi's reach as Aleksi did as he'd been ordered.

Kale swallowed the snarky remark on his tongue.

Officer Hadley was too focused on Aleksi slowly moving to where he was directed and Officer David was too concerned with groping him to notice that Barry had gotten to his knees.

Just as Kale shouted a warning, the man jumped up and ran out of the door. Both cops startled.

Aleksi moved as if to go after him.

Drawing her weapon, Officer Hadley said, "Don't move."

Kale couldn't bite his tongue this time. "Why are you pointing the gun at my body guard? The culprit is getting away."

"I decide who's the threat here," Officer Hadley snapped, her eyes cold as she pointed her gun at Aleksi.

"Let's see if you can explain that to your boss then, shall we?" Aleksi said, speaking for the first time since the police had entered the hotel suite.

Officer David removed his hand from Kale's ass and stepped away from him. "Who do you think you're talking to?"

"I'm talking to someone who will be lucky to scrape their career off the bottom of my shoe when I'm done with him." Scott McCade entered the hotel room, calm and put together. "The chief won't be pleased to know that you let the suspect get away and harassed the victim and his protection detail."

Kale hoped he wasn't the only one thinking how the hell the man knew what had happened. The two officers froze.

"I had cameras installed right after the contract was signed. I was watching from the elevator on the way up. You two"—he gestured to the officers—"just royally screwed up a case your chief—and my poker buddy—ordered you both to wrap up quickly. Hell, we set the whole thing up for you so all you had to do was arrest him, but you even blew that."

"You can't talk to us like that, *shifter*. You're nothing, so it doesn't matter what you say you saw. It will be our word against yours about what happened here. The other shifter caused a problem and became violent so we had to subdue him. Ain't that right, Hadley?"

"Sounds accurate to me, David," Officer Hadley agreed, not moving her gun away from Aleksi.

"Unfortunately, I'm the odd one in my family. I'm not a shifter," Scott said calmly.

Scott's expression changed but Kale didn't know the man well enough to judge whether it was a good thing or not.

"Did you hear enough, Chief?" Scott asked.

Kale glanced at Aleksi to see if he had any idea as to what was going on. Aleksi's face remained stoic, but as the shifter sensed Kale's attention on him, Kale saw the tiniest of smirks starting to emerge before shifter blanked his expression again.

Another man entered the room. With an average build, high cheekbones, short, dark hair and a neat goatee, the guy looked to be in his late forties. "Yes, I have. Thank you for your help, Scott. I'll see you on poker night. Mr. Andrews and his protection detail are free to go. I should tell you that I have additional uniforms waiting at the exits. The suspect was picked up and is currently being transported to the station."

With that, they were all clearly dismissed. The chief, closely followed by the two disgruntled and sweating police officers, left. Scott nodded to Aleksi and Kale then he exited as well.

Silence descended for a few minutes as Kale watched the police and Scott walk down the corridor and around the corner, out of sight. "Does this mean you have to leave too?"

He didn't want to think about why the idea of not seeing Aleksi again bothered him so much. They'd only been together a few hours. But the way the shifter didn't take any of his shit, then teased him while making him feel safe and protected—although Kale had said he didn't need nor want protection—was something he hadn't experienced before. It felt nice.

Chapter Four

Aleksi's cat was deadly quiet as they observed Kale. The model was a strange contradiction between a fashion diva, who used his looks for his own agenda, and a young man with a sharp wit and an even sharper sarcastic tongue—when he dropped the diva act. He got the feeling the real Kale was a genuine mix of the two personas he'd witnessed so far and probably had many more traits that would intrigue his beast.

"No. I'll stick around until charges are filed," he said with a shrug, playing it off as if it was no big deal.

"Oh, okay."

Kale copied Aleksi's tone but Aleksi could scent the man's relief.

"That was some performance back there." To be honest, Aleksi had half believed it himself until he'd scented Kale's disgust and embarrassment when Officer Dickhead had got too touchy-feely. Aleksi had come across his fair share of intolerant cops before and recognized Officer Dickhead for what he was—a trigger-happy bigot.

SA Welsh

"Bite me."

"Don't tempt me," he murmured.

Awkward didn't begin to sum up how...well, awkward it was as they stood there in silence, not looking at each other. Aleksi wasn't sure what to do and he hardly ever doubted himself. It was part of his cat nature to be self-assured, but Kale threw him off balance.

"So how about that beer?"

Kale startled but recovered quickly and walked in the direction of the kitchenette. "I have light beer."

"That's nothing to brag about," Aleksi growled teasingly, following him. *Damn, the male has a nice, firm ass. Those pants are practically painted on him too.*

He leaned against the counter and watched as Kale reached down into the fridge for two bottles then put them on the counter. Kale bent over to reach for something else. At that moment, Aleksi wanted nothing more than to strut over to the man and grab those two tight denim-covered globes of flesh. In his opinion, Kale was in the perfect position for it. All it would take was for him to let his claws out and carefully slash the back of Kale's jeans and Aleksi would be treated to an unfettered view of what was no doubt a drool-worthy ass.

"Aleksi!"

He shot his gaze up to meet Kale's amused, flushed face.

"The beer was the only thing I offered you."

The words were harsh, but again, Aleksi thanked his nose. Kale was embarrassed, yet interested. There was a spice of anger there too, so Aleksi backed off and held up his hands in surrender.

"Shame. I'd even choke down the fizzy alcho-pop crap if it would get me a feel of that backside." He

44

kept Kale's gaze and let the heat of his attraction show. Kale was technically no longer his protectee. No matter what he'd told Kale, the protection contract terms had been met when Barry had been arrested. Even so, Aleksi found himself willing to drink light beer in order to have an excuse to stick around.

"That must be quite the compliment coming from a manly man like yourself."

"Ah...but I'm *not* a man, though, am I?" Ordinarily, Aleksi never gave a shit what people thought of him—especially ignorant assholes like Officer Dickhead and his partner—but the little act, where Kale saved him from having to dig a bullet out of his ass, rankled his fur more than he cared to admit.

Kale froze and blushed but didn't drop his gaze. "I didn't mean it. I just didn't want you to get hurt. That guy was itching to shoot you," he defended with a tone Aleksi couldn't identify.

It might be shame, but what does the man have to be ashamed of?

The young man twisted the cap off one bottle and threw it in the sink before taking a big gulp.

Aleksi pinned Kale with a hard stare. "You let him touch you."

Kale cocked his head, furrowing his brow. "That bothered you?"

"Maybe," he admitted grudgingly.

He made himself stay perfectly still as Kale put down his beer and tentatively stepped in front of him. Breathing wasn't an option as Kale raised a hand to touch his hair.

"I...uh... Would you—?"

The moment was broken when Aleksi's phone buzzed.

Instead of crushing the damn thing, he accepted the call. "Scott?"

"Aleksi, you need to get out of there with Kale — *now*. The suspect escaped in transit, killing two officers — and there's more. When the police arrested the guy and patted him down, they found a box with a vial and a full syringe in it. Forensics are still testing it, but I recognized the name on the label. It's a powerful sedative. Whoever takes it appears conscious, but there's no one home and they have no free will. We ran the prints on the paper from the letters and the ones on the box. I had a bad feeling so I called in a favor to have them rush it and the prints match."

"Yeah, so?" What his boss had said was bad enough. But he could tell there was something more.

"*So*, it wasn't a match for Barry Mallett. Chief Morrison sent a unit to Barry's house and found the man tied up *dead* in the basement. I replaced the brother's cell and I know you took Kale's. His suite isn't safe. You need to find another location until we come up with a plan. We underestimated how far Not-Barry is willing to go."

Aleksi swore into the phone and promised to call Scott once he'd gotten Kale to safety, then he turned off the cell and removed the battery. He'd have spares at home. He wasn't going to risk that Not-Barry was techie enough to identify and trace cell signals in a specific area. His phone was the only one still on in the suite, so it wouldn't be that much of a leap if Not-Barry had managed to clone Kale's phone to receive all the information about Kale's schedule, location and communications.

"We need to leave. *Now*. Pack a bag with anything you cannot live without. You have five minutes." He took Kale's hand and pulled the man toward the bedroom, taking out his weapon and testing the weight of the 9mm in his hand as he did so.

Kale yanked his hand out of Aleksi's. Aleksi wished the human would just go along with him until he got them somewhere secure.

"What the hell is going on?" Kale demanded.

"Barry isn't Barry. He escaped and killed two cops. Plus the police have no idea where he is. So get in there and start packing. You have four minutes left to do it before I carry you out of here." Granted, he might have been a bit harsh but Not-Barry could be making his way back there right now or planning to ambush them as they left. There were too many variables.

"You're not telling me everything." Despite the stubborn tilt to his chin, Kale ran to the bedroom.

Aleksi followed, clearing the windows on his way. It was unlikely Not-Barry could manage to get access to the tenth floor suite from the outside but he wasn't going to take chances. Now that they knew Not-Barry was a killer, there were different rules to the game.

As it was, they were already behind and running a race without knowing where the finish line was. Aleksi dug his little black device out of his pocket, taped a few buttons to calibrate it to search for mics, cameras and other bugs, then tossed it to Kale.

"Wave that over everything you want to take. If it beeps, you can't take it. Whatever it is, we'll have to get it later." He could see Kale was about to argue. Aleksi tapped his watch with the gun and added, "Three minutes."

As he walked back into the main room, he heard Kale start packing. The suite was starting to feel like a lobster trap—easy to get in to and impossible to get out of.

There were only two exits he could see that Kale could take. The corridor then the stairs or the lift. Neither of those sounded like great options. It would be far too easy to set a trap to ambush them.

Aleksi could easily risk it and take out any threat that came his way, but not with his protectee. Not-Barry had already proven he was unpredictable and having his abduction scheme interrupted had probably pissed the man off. Or worse—it had made him desperate. Desperate people had nothing to lose.

It probably wasn't the best security move to open the door but it would give him a clear line of sight down the corridor to the corner. Beyond that was the set of fire doors leading to the emergency stairs. If he were Not-Barry, he would either set up the trap on the stairs or around the corner so those were out as exit points, but the lift left them trapped in a metal box with no way to see out until the doors opened, leaving Kale vulnerable. Aleksi kept half his attention on the sounds of Kale packing. He raised his eyebrows in surprise as he heard a couple of beeps. Well, shit. Not-Barry had been in the bedroom as well.

Running through the possible strategies to get out of the hotel, Aleksi decided there were only two real possibilities. One was very risky. The stairs were a death box. The other...

"I'm done," Kale announced, as he came out of the bedroom with a duffel bag.

Aleksi nodded. "Did you leave whatever beeped?"

Kale looked surprised. He clearly hadn't been around shifters much if he still didn't realize how heightened most of their senses were.

"I was going to but it's the only photo I have of my brother. I took it out of the frame and scanned it again. It didn't beep so I packed it."

"That's fine." He was impressed Kale had thought to do that. Not that he thought Kale was stupid or anything, just that civilians didn't tend to think along those lines and Aleksi knew most people would have left the photo or tried to sneak it with them regardless.

He was about to explain their options but a hiss drew his attention outside the suite. Gray smoke started clouding under the door of the stairs and was curling around the bend in the corridor wall. Their option to go upstairs was out and so was the previously discarded plan to risk the corner. He didn't like being trapped but that was exactly what Not-Barry was doing.

The gas crept closer and Aleksi sneezed then swore as his fear was confirmed — tear gas. At the moment, it wasn't close enough to do much more than make him sneeze and sting his eyes but it was getting closer.

"What's that?"

"Tear gas. Go to the window and open it as much as you can."

Kale did as instructed. Aleksi slammed the door and quickly stuffed the sofa cushions into the gap under the door to form a draft excluder. It would only give them a few more minutes reprieve from the gas before it started leaking through and around the edges of the frame.

When he joined Kale at the window, he inspected the fixings that stopped the pane opening beyond a certain point — two roll blockers, easy to disengage. Aleksi put the heel of his hand against the lock and applied a quick pop of pressure like an open-handed punch, and the stopping mechanism snapped. After repeating it with the second blocker, Aleksi then pushed the window as far open as it would go.

Just as he'd hoped, there was a small ledge about nine inches wide running under the bottom of the window and around the circumference of the building. The tenth floor wasn't exactly close to the ground but as a cat, he had no problem with heights.

"No. Absolutely not!"

Aleksi sighed, straightening from where he'd been leaning out of the window then turning back to Kale. "You don't even know what I'm going to say."

"I'm betting it involves going out that window," Kale shot back.

Aleksi didn't need his nose to tell him the man was terrified. But there wasn't any other way out that didn't involve going through the gas, and he couldn't be sure there wasn't anything nasty hissing in the smoke. After all, to get hold of that much gas in the first place implied a level of access to dangerous equipment.

"We can't get out by the stairs, because I'd be willing to bet my stash of silk cushions he's there waiting. Going farther into the gas to get around that corner and making a run for the elevator leaves us open for attack. I wouldn't be able to scent him coming, so he could grab you relatively easy. We also have no idea if he has altered the gas mix to make it more dangerous. This is the only guaranteed way out of the hotel."

He didn't share the fact that there was no guarantee that they would get out in one piece. *I just don't want to jinx some things.*

Aleksi held his hand out. "This is the only way. I'll keep you from falling. But we need to go *now*."

Kale was physically shaking and Aleksi felt sorry for him. Once Not-Barry realized they weren't going to make a run for it on the stairs or the corridor, Aleksi was sure the man would come after them in the suite.

"No. I can't. You go."

Talking was getting them nowhere. Kale still looked scared and Aleksi could hear the man's heart racing so fast Aleksi was worried the guy might faint.

"I was hired to protect you and that's what I'm going to do. Nothing is going to happen to you while I'm here. You need to trust me. Can you do that?"

Kale looked at him as if he was crazy, and if their positions were switched, Aleksi would probably think the same too.

"I…"

"If you do this, when we get to the safe house, I'll let you pet my kitty." *If in doubt, fall back on bribery.* Predatory shifters hardly ever let anyone touch them in their shifted forms and Aleksi knew Kale was curious after he'd announced what kind of cat he was at the studio.

"Really?" Kale gave him a stunning smile.

If it wasn't for the slight shake in the man's hand when he held it out, Aleksi would have been convinced he'd been played.

"Yep. Now put the bag on your back and climb out the window after me." The straps weren't likely to extend enough to fit across his shoulders.

For a moment, he was uncertain whether to wait in the suite in case Not-Barry came in or wait outside the window to stop Kale from falling. In the end, he opted for outside since Kale was so scared and he didn't want the human to slip and fall.

Stepping onto the ledge was no problem and neither was keeping his balance—it was all part of being a cat—but seeing the badly concealed look of absolute terror on Kale's face as the man gingerly climbed out of the window was awful. Kale was shaking so badly at this point that Aleksi seriously considered knocking him out and just carrying him down unconscious.

Kale narrowed his eyes. "Whatever you're thinking—hell fucking no. Climbing out of this fucking window is bad e-fucking-nough."

Well, that was certainly colorful. "You do exactly what I say and we'll get down fine. Understand?"

He knew Kale understood. However, it was psychological. If he got his protectee to say yes to a question like this, then it would create a sense of calm.

"Yes," Kale replied.

"Do you trust me?"

"I'm out on a freaking window ledge ten floors off the ground. *Yes, I trust you!*"

Aleksi hid his smile at the expression of incredulity on Kale's face. The curses were down to a minimum again—it was progress. "Good, now climb on my front like a monkey."

Kale awkwardly sidled in front of him, back as flat against the building as the bag would allow while Aleksi stood perfectly balanced with only the balls of his feet on the ledge. The man put his arms around Aleksi's neck. For a second, Aleksi contemplated stealing a kiss.

"I know that look. Stop it and concentrate. If you get us down from here in one piece, I might let you maul me, but one little bruise and I'll shave you in your sleep," Kale said with a glare.

This close to Kale, the scent of fear was easy to pick up despite his burned nostrils from the gas. They'd used up the time he'd estimated it would take to enter and fill the room, which meant Not-Barry would likely be coming to see where they were. They needed to move.

"Sounds like a deal. Wrap your legs around my waist, put your head in the curve of my neck and try to breathe normally. I'll do the rest."

Kale did as Aleksi said, carefully climbing up Aleksi's body and hesitantly hiding his face after what looked like an involuntary glance down. "You need to work on your pick-up lines," Kale said shakily.

"Why? They're clearly effective." He made sure Kale was stuck fast to his front then reached across to the insert his fingers in the grooves of the concrete. Cats loved to climb—especially his cat, when he got the chance to take a break up in the mountains.

"Asshole."

"Yes. Don't panic. Think about something else. Think about that charity thing, explain it to me." Aleksi shuffled to the column of smoother brick.

"Its…it's a group of us…models— Oh shit!"

"Easy," he crooned, as he took their combined weight on his fingers. Aleksi strained his neck to look down. *This will be a little tricky.* "Keep talking."

In a blink of an eye, he unsheathed his claws. His hands looked less cute pussy cat and not like the pansy shifters on *True Blood*—he still couldn't believe Scott had made him and the guys watch that—and more like a cross between Wolverine and Edward Scissorhands. It was definitely not something he did in public often. Humans tended to freak out—or faint.

His claws were curved like a regular cat's claws but they were so thick he had to semi-shift his hand to be able to use and control them. His fingers thickened and a strong furry webbing grew between them, supporting the stronger claws and fingers. He dug them into the concrete and grinned when they pierced it as if it was butter. It was a good thing his natural cousins had become extinct because nothing was indestructible to a saber-tooth tiger.

He curled his fingers and sank them deeper into the concrete. He toed off his shoes, unleashing his toe claws as well. As the black leather shoes plummeted to the ground, he sighed with regret. Those were great shoes. He'd picked them up from a cobbler in the Middle East.

With his claws securely dug into the wall, he carefully started to pick his way down the building, climbing the same as he would a rock cliff face. At first Kale refused to do anything but hang on for dear life and he could feel the human's heart almost hitting through his own chest.

"What's it for? Will you be prancing and writhing about in panties again?"

"I know what you're doing," Kale growled into his neck.

"I don't...know what you mean," he grunted as he lowered them the next five feet or so, much quicker this time to see if Kale could cope with it. Really, they could probably get back into the hotel through another level's window, but Aleksi's instinct was to go the whole way down like this. Thank God they were at the back of the hotel with only the almost deserted park and the lake below them. Otherwise, he'd have an ass-chewing to look forward to from Scott and the others at the office.

Shifter Equality in Life and Work—the SELW—had been burning up the pages and airwaves of the media lately, pressing the latest anti-discrimination bill that had popped into some pen pushers' heads. Aleksi didn't have anything against them, just their methods. More than one SELW activist had been caught breaking into some place or another in order to get arrested and complain about not being housed with human inmates.

Many of the SEWL policies were good and made a positive difference, but some were campaigning and picketing for the sake of it. Shifter criminals and prison inmates shouldn't be housed with humans. They were potentially too dangerous and the measures required to keep them under control would kill or damage humans. Their cuffs and restraints had to be much stronger and their cells needed to be equipped to deal with the shifters' animals. It was the same with hospitals. Sometimes a shifter was so hurt they weren't in control of themselves, the same as humans, and they deserved a safe, secure place to heal so they could be treated by doctors prepared to keep *everyone* safe until the shifter was back in his or her right mind.

He growled as he thought about his friends who had to live with the guilt of hurting someone because of ill-conceived policies. Shifters and humans were not the same, nor was one better than the other. But their differences couldn't be ignored just because someone was desperate for a cause and five minutes of fame.

As Aleksi made the jump down to the ninth floor ledge, Kale whimpered and tucked his face into his neck. He was about to comfort the man when he felt something hard pressing into his stomach.

Aleksi growled again. The man clinging to his chest shuddered and the delicious scent of arousal spiked.

"I'm a bit busy at the moment," Aleksi teased. "Can I take a rain check?"

"Bad kitty."

Aleksi laughed. "You have no idea," he said gruffly in Kale's ear. He struggled to concentrate on the job at hand as he released his claws and slid down the wall at speed.

The next few floors whooshed by in a blur as he took advantage of Kale's distraction to hurry their descent. He took care to growl and shamelessly purr when Kale's lust dampened under the weight of fear.

"You're cheating," Kale accused, sounding annoyed. But that didn't stop him from pulling Aleksi tighter.

It might have been Aleksi's wishful thinking, but he swore he felt Kale's teeth graze his shoulder through his shirt. "So are you," he retorted breathlessly.

He felt Kale shrug. "All's fair…"

Once Aleksi reached the fourth floor ledge, he checked the distance to the ground below. Grinning, he let go of the wall with one hand and cupped the back of Kale's head, encouraging the man to look up at him. "Do you still trust me?"

Kale's eyes shot wide and his heart raced. "No. I've changed my mind."

If anyone asked, he would say his cat made him do it, but in reality, he thought it would do Kale good to live a little on the wild side. The man was entirely too well put together. Aleksi laughed cheerfully before letting go of the building and jumping away from the wall, curling his arms around Kale as the man screamed.

"Too late," Aleksi said.

They landed with a solid thud, his feet claws treading the earth and grass as his knees bent to absorb the impact. "That was fun, huh?"

Kale gave him a glare, which clearly said Aleksi had a few screws loose, and tried to catch his breath. "Ass. Hole."

Aleksi smirked, the expression turning to a wide smile when Kale made no move to get off him. Perhaps he should jump off buildings more often.

Daring his luck, Aleksi gave Kale's firm ass a smack. They needed to get moving. It wasn't safe here. The smack worked. Kale dropped to his feet and glowered at him before flipping off Aleksi and muttering something about bloody cats and their psychotic tendencies.

He was sure Kale realized he could hear him. A scowl from Kale confirmed it and more muttering followed. It was good to know he was a 'stupid, handsome, idiotic, hot shifter with muscles bigger than planets'. His protectee was surely in shock.

"Hey, my shoes." They lay only a few feet away, looking none the worse for wear after the ten-story drop. At least one thing had gone right today.

The road ahead led into the park and the alley behind them led back onto the main street. The park would give them cover, but the street would give them more options for transport.

"This way." Aleksi herded Kale into the alley.

He looked up and saw a figure leaning out of Kale's window. Aleksi was certain that Not-Barry wasn't going to give up on getting Kale any time soon.

* * * *

"I can't believe you stole a car!" Kale shouted for the second time. He was now an accessory to a crime.

"Will you get over it already? I'll call Scott and have him send someone to pick it up where we left it then return it to the owner." Aleksi rolled his eyes as if grand theft auto wasn't a big deal.

Kale wasn't convinced.

His shifter bodyguard might kill him quicker than his stalker would. Jumping off a building—what was he thinking? Then slapping his ass like he had. It had been bad enough getting another inappropriate erection. Any rational person would be terrified when they were one wrong move away from plummeting to their deaths. At least *he* was. Kale was certain the saber-tooth tiger shifter would have landed on his feet, like any other cat.

The manic smile of excitement the big shifter had given him right before stepping off that last ledge would be forever burned in his memory. And the next time Aleksi asked Kale to trust him, he was answering what he should have in the first place—hell and no.

Aleksi had stolen a car then he'd driven for over an hour before abandoning the vehicle at the side of the road and making the hike on foot through thick woodland. When they stopped, there was a small clearing where the trees didn't intrude on a small, neatly kept garden. A paved path that had a mosaic effect of pastel blue and green in swirling patterns lead up to a two-story house that had green wooden shutters and an old-fashioned, dark-green stable door. Despite those things, the house appeared modern and...homey.

"What do you think?"

"This doesn't look like a safe house." He frowned as Aleksi retrieved a key from a hollowed-out log that lay with planted herbs under the kitchen window.

"Been to many, have you?"

"Well...no. But it doesn't look like how I imagined one to look—cold and unfriendly. This is lovely. A family could live here with a dog and have barbeques in the summers on the log burner over there." Sure enough there was a wood-burning grill in a shaded corner of the garden that he could imagine cooking on.

When the shifter didn't reply, Kale turned to see the much bigger man staring at him. "What?"

"I didn't expect you to like it. You're a city boy." Kale didn't get a chance to respond, as Aleksi opened the door and went inside. He followed the shifter and frowned again when Aleksi toed off the shoes they'd retrieved from the hotel garden and placed them on a shoe rack to the left of the door in the small porch that seemed to double as a mud room for boots and coats.

"Wait. This is *your* house?" Kale examined everything with new eyes. The soft furnishings created a comfy and cozy ambience and the relaxed style of the worn black leather sofa and armchairs made Kale feel like he wasn't a stranger but a welcomed guest. The contrast of the sleek, modern kitchen with the black marble countertops and stainless-steel appliances—such as the fridge, toaster, oven and microwave—was reflective of the big, bad bodyguard and the playful cat shifter who had teased him then smacked his ass. It just…fit him.

"Yes. I don't get to stay here as much as I'd like since my job takes me all over the world, but this is where I call home." Aleksi led him away from the kitchen and living room to a set of dark-stained wooden stairs.

"We're going upstairs?"

"Yes. So I can show you where you'll be sleeping and you can wash that glittery stuff off. You look like an extra from that Twitchy franchise."

The way Aleksi said it made him laugh. Manly men really had a thing about glitter. It was as if the substance automatically castrated them or something.

"Twitchy? Do you mean *Twilight*?" He wasn't even touching the comment about the makeup he still wore.

Aleksi seemed completely undaunted by the fact Kale was a model. Although the shifter gave him signals that suggested he was interested, Kale wondered if it was simply because of how he looked or whether someone finally liked him for him. They hadn't known each other long enough for it to be his personality. The thought disappointed him more than he'd expected.

"Yeah," Aleksi answered, smirking in a way that told Kale the shifter had gotten it wrong on purpose to see if Kale knew it well enough to recognize it by the wrong name. Sneaky.

"Ass."

"So you keep saying. Do you know any other curses or has all the pretty sparkly vampire drama addled your mind?" Aleksi teased with a wink.

Kale pushed past the annoying shifter and stormed up the stairs. He ignored the fact that Aleksi *let* Kale shove him. Kale was secure in his manhood, but it annoyed him sometimes that Aleksi was so much stronger.

"You know... You're pretty enough to be one of those sparkly characters in that bunch of vampire films. Except not the one who looks like he cried in his Cheerios every morning." Aleksi shadowed his steps.

Kale tried to get rid of the blush creeping up his neck.

"Thank you." Hopefully Aleksi would drop the topic. It didn't annoy him at all that he evidently *wasn't* pretty enough as the casting director had chosen they guy with the eyebrows instead. Nope, not one bit. "So which room did you say I was staying in?"

"I'm the first on the left and you're right next door."

It was hard to miss the way Aleksi narrowed his eyes in interest as the cat noticed the change of subject. Kale was beginning to feel like prey around the powerful shifter.

Once Aleksi had shown Kale to his room, they went back downstairs and fixed something to eat. Despite the impressive kitchen, it seemed Aleksi's signature dish was canned tomato soup and grilled cheese sandwiches. He was doubtful at first, picking at the melted cheese, but Kale was surprised at how nice the meal was.

Aleksi had made a remark about him being too prissy to eat grilled cheese.

The comment had hit home.

He remembered, just a few weeks ago, that Caleb had asked him to help out with landscaping at his new house. Kale had thought it was a joke at the time and he'd offered his brother the number of a professional, as if it was ludicrous to think that *he*, a successful model, would ever dig in the mud to clean out the old lake.

When his modeling career had taken off, he'd been swept away in the lifestyle that went with it in fancy soirees and dining out at restaurants more nights than not. Somewhere along the way, he'd forgotten where he'd come from.

Later, as he sat on the bed looking out of the window at the night sky, he appreciated the stars he couldn't see in the city. Now that he was thinking about it, he recalled at least half a dozen instances where he saw how he'd let his brother down. He'd always thought he wasn't like the prima donna models he worked with whose lives revolved around artificial things and their appearance.

Kale rubbed his stomach in an attempt to ease the heavy feeling there.

Perhaps it was time to reevaluate his life.

Movement outside the window caught his eye and he gasped at what he saw. Aleksi stood stark naked in the middle of the backyard, looking up at Kale's window as if he wanted Kale to see him.

The man was truly magnificent.

He wasn't close enough to see the details of the shifter's no doubt perfect body, but even from where he sat in the guest room, Kale was impressed with every part of the man—especially the more generous area.

Aleksi didn't move and Kale took advantage of the fact to ogle him longer, but too soon, the man turned around. Then it was as if his skin burst apart to reveal a massive saber-tooth tiger. The beast was nothing like the one from *Ice Age*. This was a dangerous, scary creature that could probably reach his window if it stood on its back legs.

It was as if Aleksi had heard his thoughts, as one moment he was looking out at the night and the next, the enormous face of a saber-tooth tiger filled the large window as Aleksi reared up on his hind legs.

Kale stumbled and hit the bed hard, tumbling backward. Trying to catch himself only made things worse and he rolled off the bed, landing with a crash and a yelp.

The cat's breath fogged the glass and it nudged the pane with its big, pinkish-brown nose as though he wanted Kale to open it.

"Uh-uh. Maybe…maybe next time," he forced out numbly.

The tiger mewled and prodded the glass again with its nose. Instead of being the harmless gesture the shifter probably thought it was, all it did was draw Kale's attention to the massive front teeth that were bigger than Kale's arms as they tapped the window.

Kale frowned at the tiger, trying to convince himself that he wasn't on the verge of having a panic attack.

"It's not happening, Aleksi."

The cat huffed and stuck its big pink tongue out to lick the transparent surface before moving away, making chuffing sounds as it left. Kale got the feeling Aleksi was laughing at him.

"I hope you get fleas!"

A small roar of what he guessed was indignation sounded from outside then it all went quiet.

Being face-to-face or touching Aleksi's animal was going to take a bit of working up to. He climbed to his feet and headed to the bathroom to get ready for bed, but he paused for a minute to take a sneak peek out of the window. Aleksi had gone but his massive paw prints remained. Kale gulped. *A whole lot of working up to.*

* * * *

If Kale *was* still there come morning, Aleksi would admit to being wrong about him. Sticking around after coming face to face with his beast would convince Aleksi that Kale was more than he pretended to be. He'd seen flashes of a man Aleksi was curious to get to know and he was interested in pursuing the attraction with him after this was over, but those flashes were smothered by a façade. He'd bet the real Kale didn't even realize the superior attitude came up as a wall.

At dinner, the way the man had wrinkled his nose at Aleksi's choice of meal had poked at the part of Aleksi that was still the scared little boy on the streets of Russia trying to get enough to eat. That was before Scott's brother, Robert, had found him and brought him home to America. He knew he was sensitive about it, but seeing Kale's model persona sneer at the food he shared with him had pissed off Aleksi more than he wanted to admit to himself. So, he had let it fester away until he'd deliberately pushed the human too far. Aleksi never just unleashed his animal around a stranger. It was too dangerous for them both.

Not that he would hurt anyone, but he would defend himself.

Kale had actually taken it really well, despite the putrid smell of fear. The guy hadn't run from him screaming—which was a lot more than some had done when faced with his cat.

If Kale did run, Aleksi would be there to protect the human from the other predators in the woods. If not, he would apologize in the morning.

Guarding the house, Aleksi settled his big head on his front paws.

* * * *

Aleksi plated up the apple pancakes and glanced for the hundredth time in the direction of the stairs. It was a little past nine and Kale still hadn't come down, despite Aleksi having heard him get out of the shower an hour ago.

Just as he was ready to go up and get the man, he heard the top step creak.

He busied himself with making tea as he pretended he wasn't listening to Kale coming closer and entering the kitchen.

"Morning."

"Morning," Kale answered.

Aleksi stirred in enough milk to take out the natural bitterness of the tealeaves and removed the strainer, setting it aside. He turned and offered Kale one of the cups.

With a gasp of pleasure, Kale quickly took it and smiled gratefully. "How did you know I preferred tea to coffee?"

He hid his smile behind his cup as he blew across the surface of the hot liquid. "I didn't. I prefer it myself."

Kale blushed beautifully. "Oh. Thank you for sharing some."

"You're welcome."

They settled into an awkward silence and moved to sit at opposite ends of the table in the kitchen-diner, not looking at each other. There were few things Aleksi hated more than apologizing for doing something wrong. It was easier when he knew he was right, because he could just fake it.

"I wanted to apologize for scaring you last night. I was wrong." The humble pie burned going down. Aleksi stared into his mug, watching the steam swirling in patterns on the air above the hot liquid. When he didn't get any kind of a response, he steeled himself and raised his head.

Kale was looking at him with a strange expression. "Thank you. Something tells me it was my mouth that struck first." He shrugged sheepishly. "I'm sorry too."

Aleksi dropped his gaze to Kale's lips and his cat stirred. He knew Kale had noticed he was staring, but Aleksi couldn't seem to look away from the pink lips that were blushing red as Kale bit the bottom one. Apologizing didn't seem easy for either of them.

Aleksi inclined his head. "I suppose I'm sensitive about certain topics."

"And sometimes I'm a bitch. I didn't realize how much I've changed since becoming a successful model. I must have let the hype get to me. I'll rein it in. Whatever I said, I'm sorry."

The humor of their situation struck him and he laughed, finally able to look away from Kale's mouth. "Are we arguing about who was an ass first?"

Kale smiled back, relaxing his shoulders. "Yes, I guess we are. Truce?"

Aleksi didn't hesitate for a second before grasping the hand Kale held out to him. He let go then motioned to the pancakes he'd made earlier. He was starving.

"They should still be warm. Dig in."

"No, thank you. If I eat even a quarter of what's there, I'll have to work out like demon before the Paris shoot the day after tomorrow." Despite his words, though, Aleksi could see the longing for the sugary goodness of pancakes, bacon and syrup.

"Can't you treat yourself?"

"My career is my looks, and fashion designers are always demanding skinnier models. I'm established, so I get a little leeway with my weight as long as the muscles don't get too big or too small. But no sugar or fatty foods for me until I retire, I'm afraid." Kale sent another wistful look in the direction of the pancakes before grabbing a granola bar from his pocket with a sigh. Even the packet looked unappealing. No sugar, fat, color or flavor. Now that was the way to sell a product.

"That sucks. I don't get why they think bones are hot. Eat your fill, then I'll take you on a run in the woods. I guarantee you'll work it off." Aleksi didn't mention that shifters ran much faster and had greater stamina so he could go all day—all night too—but under different circumstances. When he was finished with Kale, the man would be a sweaty mess.

Mmm. Kale all nice and sweaty, body strained from exhaustion and endorphins. *Now that's a nice mental image.*

"Really? I've never gotten into running. Didn't see the point unless you were running away from something."

"I could always chase you." He threw it out there as a joke, but the immediate burst of excitement coming off Kale surprised him. *Interesting.*

He narrowed his eyes and took a deliberate deep breath, letting Kale know he was scenting him. The guy blushed a delightful pink. Aleksi was about to blow off the joke in case Kale spooked but again, the man surprised him. He really should remember that Kale wasn't a normal human.

"Umm. Sure?"

* * * *

Kale stopped running as he got back to the house. He bent over, bracing his hands on his knees, and tried to drag in enough air to get his lungs to stop his body screaming for oxygen. Sweat trickled into his eyes. "I...hate...you," he wheezed.

"Hey, I gave you to choice of going easy." Aleksi, the evil, sadistic shifter, jogged up to him, barely out of breath.

"And you made it clear you would be bored to tears with that option," Kale shot back, wishing he'd gone with the easy option. He'd wanted to impress Aleksi, but now he wanted to collapse in to a weeping ball of ouch.

Aleksi's feet came into his view. "Come on. Let's get you into a warm bath."

Kale let himself be led and didn't resist when the shifter wrapped an arm around his waist as they walked the short distance to the house together. He couldn't even enjoy it. By the time they reached the door, Kale was sweating even more as parts of his body started to freeze up from the sudden shock of overuse.

Aleksi pulled him inside, but before they got to the stairs, Kale's knees stopped cooperating and he had to shout. "Stop. I can't. Just let me sit for a minute."

"You need to soak your muscles or they'll lock."

He knew he had pushed himself too far. And the effort to impress Aleksi had completely backfired. His humiliation was complete as the bigger man scooped him up off the floor into solid, unyielding arms.

"Don't look like that. I can't believe you ran so far. Why didn't you say you were struggling?"

This close, and with his face level with Aleksi's chin, he couldn't hide what he was feeling from him, so he ducked his head and refused to meet the man's eyes. What had he been thinking? Even if he hadn't almost keeled over, the man just wasn't interested. Aleksi had been all but unaffected by him and had made it clear that the fact that Kale was a model didn't impress him one bit.

* * * *

Kale still hadn't managed to shake the unfamiliar feeling of shyness for Aleksi as, several minutes later, the shifter helped him sink into a hot, vanilla-scented bubble bath. "Oh man, that's good." Kale sank all the way up to his neck and his feet still didn't touch the end of the tub.

"Now I have you at my mercy. Tell me truthfully, why you did this to yourself?"

The relaxing effect of the bath took away some of the sting to his pride, but it added a whole different kind of hurt as Aleksi stripped off his shirt and threw it in the laundry hamper. The shifter perched on the side of the free-standing claw-foot bath. With a thin sheen of sweat covering his chest, Aleksi was stunning. Kale usually liked his men with little or no hair on their chests, but he had to admit the blond curls were tempting. It made him wonder what sort of noises the shifter would make if he tugged on them.

Thankfully, Aleksi had been generous with the bubble bath and his dick was covered as he came to full arousal. But that wouldn't stop the shifter from picking it up from his scent if he didn't get a hold of himself.

"I don't know, I guess I wanted to impress you or something." He settled on the noncommittal answer and prayed Aleksi would leave it alone. He should have known better, though. A cat with a puzzle was worse than a dog with a bone.

Aleksi frowned and Kale inwardly groaned. Where was his usual charm and confidence? "Why would you want to impress me?"

"So you wouldn't ask that question?" He laughed at Aleksi's confused expression. "I like you, okay? I know you know I'm attracted to you. Hell, who wouldn't be? But you don't seem to notice me other than to protect me. You don't even like me." Saying it stung was an understatement, but Kale wasn't going to beg for anyone's attention.

"We only met yesterday. I don't know you well enough to like you or dislike you."

Kale gestured, inadvertently flicking soap at Aleksi and laughed depreciatingly. "There you go, then." As soon as he was done with this protection shit, he was going to the nearest club and picking up a host of men to make him forget about the shifter in front of him.

"I wasn't finished."

Aleksi tried to touch his hand but Kale evaded him. No doubt the shifter was going to try to let him down easy as if he were some blushing virgin with a crush. No thanks.

"Are you going to list the reasons why someone like you would never be interested in someone like me? Because if you are, you can skip it." He closed his eyes, held his breath and sank under the bubbles. A childish move, but one that let him keep what remained of his self-respect. The only problem was that he would eventually have to come back up for air.

Kale stayed under until he really had to breathe again. But when he emerged from out of the water, the shifter was gone. He sighed. He'd chased off another one. If he'd kept his mouth shut, they might have ended up friends. Instead, he'd managed to ruin that too by acting like a child having a tantrum.

"You have issues," Aleksi pointed out bluntly, reentering the bathroom with a glass of green liquid.

He frowned and curled his lip. "Thanks."

"You are high maintenance, prissy, stubborn, moody, in denial that you're in danger and you have trouble listening to people. You rely on your looks to get what you want, you run away from dealing with your problems and most of all, you don't eat sugar. What's up with that?" The Americanism was set off nicely by the faintest hint of a Russian accent.

Kale blinked. He'd been joking when he'd mentioned Aleksi listing his faults.

The shifter growled, probably at his lack of response or reaction.

Before he had a chance to move away or say something stupid, the big blond shifter claimed his mouth. He tried to pull away and ask what the hell Aleksi was doing, but the shifter cupped the back of Kale's head in one big hand, keeping Kale there. And really, why would he want to get away?

It started off slowly, with Aleksi teasing his lips, and when he opened for the shifter, Aleksi dominated, demanding and powerful. Kale's thoughts of friendship fizzled out under the masterful ministrations. The second his tongue was stroked by Aleksi's, his dwindling erection came back to life full force.

The kiss turned desperate as Kale reached up to clutch at Aleksi's big, muscular shoulders. He couldn't get any purchase in the tub so all he could do was try to urge the shifter closer. Aleksi was solid and unmoving, though, and Kale mewled in frustration. He needed Aleksi to touch him. If this was the only chance he was going to get at Aleksi before the shifter remembered all the bad things he'd listed, then Kale was damn well going to make the most of it.

Thankfully, Aleksi took pity on him. Kale heard the clink of the glass being put down, then Aleksi sank his hand into the bubbles and took hold of him. "Oh, fuck."

"Not yet," Aleksi spoke into his mouth.

Kale was so hot for Aleksi that it was embarrassing. No one had ever pushed his buttons the way this man did. He keened when Aleksi squeezed him tightly and arched his hips to get more of that touch. "Uh!"

He dove back into the kiss, smiling into it when Aleksi startled him and took control again. A deep growl rumbled through Aleksi's chest and into Kale's. Aleksi lifted him up out of the water just enough to press their bare torsos together. With Kale's skin wet and soapy from the bath, it gave enough slick for him to slide against Aleksi's wide chest, teasing them both by stimulating their nipples with the slippery rubbing.

Moaning, Kale trusted Aleksi to keep him aloft and trailed his hands from Aleksi's shoulders, down his sides, then slid them around to graze his fingernails over the shifter's back.

Aleksi howled and started jerking Kale's cock faster, holding him up with one arm.

He retaliated by moving his hands down to Aleksi's waistband and dipped under the belt and fabric. The belt gave way as he pulled the tooth out of the hole, making short work of the button and zip fly as well. Aleksi's hard cock sprang out—the whole ten inches or so by the feel of it—and almost so thick he couldn't close his hand around it fully.

Kale's gasp was half fearful and half lustful. Something that big would hurt if the owner didn't take care of the person they were with.

It was a struggle to choose between kissing Aleksi's lips or seeing the large cock in his hand and giving his partner pleasure. Just the thought of making big, bad and totally controlled Aleksi lose it was intoxicating. He wanted to see Aleksi fly apart and come all over his hand.

"Please."

Aleksi released him from the kiss but Kale had to struggle not to simply sink back into the hot water and let Aleksi have his way. Never had someone kissing his neck taken him to the edge before. This wasn't some hook-up, though. He actually liked Aleksi, and Kale wanted to please him.

He got a better grip, using his one hand to fist up and down the length of Aleksi's cock and the other to scoop up some of the bubbles from the bath to ease the way. Once he'd wet his hand and Aleksi's dick enough to set a faster rhythm, he concentrated his efforts on thumbing the reddened head and leaking slit. When Aleksi replaced the lips on his neck with his teeth—the barest touch of teeth and a guttural moan from the shifter—Kale knew he was close.

"Come for me," Kale ordered.

He waited for the split second Aleksi's eyes flashed to his and turned cat before he moved his hand down to Aleksi's heavy balls and squeezed gently.

Aleksi roared and came over Kale's hand. The man was beautiful in ecstasy. And those green and gold cat eyes were trained on him through it all. Being the center of someone's world, even in their pleasure, was overwhelming and he couldn't hold himself back when Aleksi struck, slamming their lips together.

All through his climax, Aleksi milked Kale's erection until he was spent and limp.

When the kiss ended, they were both breathing heavily and Kale saw Aleksi's cock start to fill and grow again. *That is a very quick recovery time, impressively quick.* Kale raised his head and smiled seductively at Aleksi, but the shifter didn't take the bait. Instead, he got up and tucked himself back in his pants. The endorphins that had blocked the pain from Kale's abused muscles were creeping back in, but he had no doubt Aleksi could find a way to get his endorphins pumping again.

Instead, Aleksi shoved the glass of green goo at him. "Drink this."

Kale took it without thinking, still dazed from the kiss. "What's in it?" He sniffed the glass and almost gagged at the strong, raw, herby scent. Even the weight of the glass resting on his knee was painful. It was so much better when Aleksi was kissing him, so why couldn't the shifter just accept a life of sexual slavery and kiss Kale forever? *Selfish shifter.*

"Family secret."

Kale plugged his nose and drank the foul stuff down, and damn if he didn't feel better after a few breaths. He could almost feel the muscles in his arms and legs sigh in relief and the knotted, overworked muscles unclenched and loosened enough that Kale didn't have to bite his tongue to keep the cries of pain quiet.

"Feel better?" Even though it was a question, it was clear Aleksi knew the answer.

"I still hate you."

"No, you don't. You think I'm smexy," Aleksi said confidently.

Kale handed the empty glass back and Aleksi put it on the counter by the sink.

"Smexy isn't a word," he argued.

"Yes, it is. My last protectee taught it to me. It means smart and sexy — smexy."

Before he lost his courage, Kale asked the question that had been bugging him for the last few minutes. "Can I ask you something?"

Aleksi cocked his head. "Sure."

"Did we really get each other off? Because it seems like you're unaffected. If you don't want to take it any further — that's fine — but I would like to know one way or the other, please?" It was odd being on this end of the conversation. His usual hookups all knew the score and weren't looking for anything more than a warm bedmate for the night, but there had been a couple over the years who had changed their minds in the morning.

For a moment, Kale thought Aleksi wasn't going to answer, then the man sighed deeply. Aleksi sat on the side of the tub again and reached out to pick up his hand. Kale let the man hold his hand and frowned. He'd never indulged in casual touches from a lover before, but he found he liked it.

"It is not that I do not want you—clearly I do. Predatory shifters in general find it harder to get close to their lovers because to lose them would leave them vulnerable. I know you are leaving once Not-Barry is apprehended by the police. Yet I could not stop myself from touching you." That hint of accent was back again and his informal ease of vocabulary had diminished.

"I don't get close to people, either. It seems crazy that we only met yesterday but I really feel as if I've known you for much longer. Recently I've realized I need to make some changes in my life. Otherwise, I'll lose the person I was before all the glitter and spotlights. I'm scared, but I would like to see if we could have something real, something we could build on after this mess with Not-Barry is over." By the end of his speech, Kale was staring at their joined hands, unable to keep Aleksi's piercing gaze. He hated putting himself out there and most of all he hated the timid feeling it gave him. One thing he wasn't was timid.

They settled into silence, but it wasn't altogether uncomfortable, only tense as he waited for Aleksi to say something.

"I will agree to see where this goes only if you promise to be honest about the important things."

"The important things," he agreed eagerly. It was a reasonable demand.

"And a promise from you that you will not simply run away if things become hard to deal with."

He didn't like the sound of that, but the look Aleksi gave him had him biting down on his defensive, snarky comments.

"Fine. Deal."

Aleksi looked him dead in the eye then nodded, smiling so brightly it lit up the man's rough features and made him look only a few years older than Kale. Now he was glad he hadn't spoiled that sight with a stupid half-assed comment.

"Will you get in here with me?" He swooshed his hands in the bubbles in invitation. The warm water was lovely.

Aleksi hesitated. "I should call Scott for an update."

Kale wasn't above begging. Something inside him just wanted to be close to the shifter, needed to be close, but he wasn't ready to look at that need too closely. Agreeing to honesty and promising not to run was as fast as he was willing to go with this budding relationship right now. *Holy shit, I'm in a relationship.*

He shoved the shock aside and focused on getting Aleksi to stay with him. "Please?"

"Only for a little while," Aleksi conceded.

Kale scooted forward to leave room for Aleksi to squeeze in behind him once he stripped off his pants, underwear and boots. The water level rose, swelling to the brim.

"The water might spill over," he warned.

"That's okay. The boards are old but strong, they can take a little water." Aleksi kissed his ear, gently pulling him so Kale's back rested against Aleksi's front.

Sighing, Kale let the last of the tension in him float away. He knew Aleksi wouldn't let him drown since it wouldn't look good for the whole bodyguard image.

He relaxed in Aleksi's hold and trailed his fingers up and down Aleksi's forearms. "So…how about we give introducing me to your tiger another go?"

Chapter Five

As they stood outside, Aleksi wasn't sure this was such a good idea. He hadn't exactly introduced Kale to his tiger in the most careful of ways and the last thing he wanted was for his lover to run from him— especially when his tiger could think they were playing a game and chase after Kale.

He didn't want to call Kale *his* human yet. Despite the mutual pleasure they'd found in the bath yesterday, they were taking it slow. The more dominant and predatory the animal half of the shifter was, the more danger a prospective mate was in. Aleksi wasn't going to make the leap or let his cat become too attached to Kale until he knew they had something more than just attraction between them.

"Kale..."

Kale called him on his attempt to delay shifting. "Stop stalling and show me. I swear I won't run and I'll do everything you told me to do. I won't approach you until you come to me first, I won't stare into your eyes and most importantly, I won't run."

Aleksi had perfect control of his cat but the feral instincts were still there and he didn't want to take any chances with Kale. Knowing Kale wasn't going to let him put this off much longer, he sighed. "Okay."

There wasn't a big ceremony or the horror show writhing in pain where bones popped and snapped. Aleksi's shift was seamless. One minute he stood in his man form and the next, his tiger burst free. If he had to describe how the process felt, he would liken it to stretching out all his muscles after a long sleep in a small space or after a very long drive. It felt good—freeing—and gave him a jolt of energy.

He lifted his head high and roared happily, chuffing when the forest birds chirped and flew into the air in answer. Perhaps he'd go and chase them later. He hadn't done that for a while.

"Oh. Fuck."

The whispered curse drew his attention and he snapped his gaze over to the little man. The cat part of his brain assessed Kale as a potential meal but quickly rejected the idea of eating the nice-smelling human.

Aleksi drew in a deep breath, analyzing the scents until he filtered out all the irrelevant information and focused on the human's scent. There was fear there—a good amount of it—but that wasn't new. Everyone feared him. However, there was also something else. It wasn't pleasure or surprise. It was something new, something he hadn't identified before in this form.

He stepped forward slowly so as not to startle the human and crouched when he got within a few feet of Kale. What would the human do next?

He didn't have to wait long to find out as Kale took a hesitant step toward him, head down in a submissive gesture that Aleksi appreciated. He made an encouraging sound and the human's gaze flicked up to his, eyes wide before looking quickly away again.

Thankfully, his tiger had no interest in declaring dominance over Kale so Aleksi loosened the reins of his control a little, letting his animal nature interact more freely with his new lover.

Non-shifters never understood the relationship a shifter had with their animal. It was a part of them, *was* them, but at the same time, it was something wild with a will of its own. Dominant predatory shifters were taught from birth to keep an iron control over their animals. Otherwise, there would be a deep conflict inside them that often left the shifter mad, dead or hunted down for the good of others. Even though he'd only had a few years with his family before they'd died, Aleksi remembered that first lesson.

Once an understanding was reached between animal and man personalities, shifters became whole. If that balance wasn't reached, then they had a problem.

Aleksi stayed where he was and Kale closed the distance between them. He made a soft trill, the cat equivalent of hello, and gently pressed his nose into Kale's middle. The size difference between them meant he had to be very careful not to hurt Kale, but when Kale brought his hand up to smooth behind his ear, all bets were off. Aleksi pushed more forcefully against Kale and huffed when he accidentally knocked the human back onto his ass.

With careful movements, he crawled forward and placed his big head in Kale's lap. He mindfully turned his head so his extended canines didn't inadvertently cause damage to his lover.

"Umm. Are you asking for more scritches?"

He made an assenting noise like a chirp and rubbed his cheek on Kale's legs.

Kale must have understood because he started the lovely petting again. It wasn't long before a rumbling purr started in his chest, making the human beneath him vibrate too, but Kale didn't stop smoothing and rubbing him. Aleksi closed his eyes and let the attention soothe him.

* * * *

Aleksi finished buttoning his pants and looked at Kale, who looked as relaxed as Aleksi felt. He was still stunned that Kale had stayed with him and had indulged his cat. No one had ever done that before. Everyone got scared and left. Even Scott and his friends, who he loved as brothers, got twitchy around his tiger.

Searching for something to say, Aleksi wrapped his arms around Kale's waist, bringing their bodies together. He wasn't the only one getting aroused now that he had shifted back. "My tiger will know you next time, so you won't have to be as formal."

"So he likes me?"

Kale sounded so hopeful Aleksi couldn't smother the laugh bubbling up from his chest. "Yes, he likes you."

"Good. Want to take a bath?"

Aleksi knew neither of them was concerned about the dirt and autumn leaves sticking to their clothes. He smiled, letting his teeth show in a predatory smile. "Definitely." Kale giggled then broke free of the embrace and ran toward the house.

"Last one in has to do the dishes later," Kale shouted back, laughing as he entered the house.

Aleksi laughed too before chasing after the silly human.

* * * *

Aleksi observed the Parisian crowds gathered around taking pictures of the Eiffel Tower. People oohed and aahed and clicked photo after photo. He had to admit that it was impressive. He'd never had the opportunity to see it in all its glory before. His previous visits to Paris had been at night and had only required him to stay a few hours in order to complete a job.

Kale stood beside him, just as taken with the beauty as the rest of the tourists. Their flight to Milan left in a few hours. They really didn't have time to sightsee, but Kale had really wanted to visit this place. The photo shoot hadn't run on as long as the one with Philippe had, so Aleksi had caved and said they could come here on the way to the airport. Their car was waiting for them nearby and Aleksi was ready to bundle up Kale and run like a quarterback to safety.

"Thank you for this," Kale said softly, reaching out to take his hand as he kept staring at the tourist tower.

"You're welcome." Aleksi looked down at their joined hands and smiled.

* * * *

Aleksi watched the crowds, scanning them for any indication of a threat. Something wasn't sitting right with him. The day before in Paris had gone smoothly and he'd spotted nothing to suggest that they were being watched or followed. Scott and the police hadn't found anything to suggest that Not-Barry had followed them to Paris or to where they were now in Milan. No one matching the description had been reported as flying to either France or Italy.

But there was something not quite right.

Someone as dedicated to his obsession as Not-Barry wouldn't simply give up. Scott had called before they'd left for Milan to say that Not-Barry's fingerprints had come back and had been flagged as a person of interest in three other murders in the last two years — all high-profile people, either on television or in magazines. The police had also been contacted by the FBI, saying they wanted to be kept in the loop regarding Not-Barry. In his experience with the FBI, they were great at tracking people, but not that good with sharing the information with others. Competition between the alphabet agencies was still alive and kicking. The FBI were keen on being kept in the loop with this, which suggested that Not-Barry had information they wanted. They must intend to offer the man a deal, probably immunity.

After this, they had a one-night stopover before flying out to New York for a charity job Kale had spoken of in the beginning. Aleksi knew the man was looking forward to event by the animated way Kale talked about it.

The travel times were ridiculous. They barely had enough time to catch their breaths before having to make another appointment. This wasn't exactly the glamorous champagne-and-leisure lifestyle he'd imagined models lived. Kale seemed used to the running around, though, and he didn't hear the man complain once.

They'd arrived in Milan hours ago and had gone straight to the fashion show where the creative director had told Kale he would be opening and closing the event. Aleksi guessed that was an important thing because Kale had practically been buzzing after the news.

The security for the fashion show had been eyeballing him since they'd gotten here. The head of the team wasn't buying that Aleksi was here as an overprotective boyfriend. Ironically enough, that part was now true, but it wasn't the whole truth.

As he watched Kale getting ready, he tried not to glare at the dressers and assistants pawing at his lover. They had agreed not to sleep together until Not-Barry was caught. Both of them were afraid of being burned and didn't want to be too invested if things went badly.

That didn't mean they weren't having as many *baths* as Kale could stand. Their time at his house hadn't been long enough. Aleksi wanted to keep the model there indefinitely, where he would be safe, but even he realized that was a no-go.

He growled as the overly helpful dressing assistant tried to cop a feel while helping Kale into some weird getup that convinced Aleksi he knew nothing about fashion. What he was seeing looked more like a DIY Halloween costume gone wrong. It had ribbon and…bits hanging off wire almost a foot from Kale's bare torso. Even squinting and cocking his head to the side didn't yield any view he considered good. This really was a completely different world.

Aleksi smirked as Kale batted the grabbing hand away and, with a single scathing look, sent the assistant running.

The male model next to Kale stopped preening and posing in front of the mirror. "Too good for a pre-show suck-off?" To make the crude point, the model gripped the head of one of his dressers and pushed the guy toward his groin, thrusting for show.

"No. Too good to be mauled like a club slut—or to behave like one." Kale didn't even look in the other model's direction as he delivered the verbal blow. Aleksi's lover could do bitchy quite well, it seemed.

The model's face flushed red with anger and he shoved the willing assistant off him, taking a step toward Kale. "Now I *know* a stuck-up princess like you needs a good, hard fucking. I'll bet you haven't had that itch scratched in a long time, princess."

Aleksi lost his humor and came forward, standing next to Kale so the model could see he was more than capable of satisfying Kale—and squashing the asshole like an annoying bug.

"That won't be necessary. I take care of any *itches* Kale has."

The forward model quickly turned on the spot and marched away from them, followed by his posse of dressers.

Kale touched his arm and blew him a kiss. "Thanks, honey."

"Aww," the gaggle of assistants and dressers sang together.

Aleksi had momentarily forgotten about the crowd watching them. Even the other models looked amused by the asshole's departure.

Only Aleksi seemed to recognize the anger in Kale's eyes. The other assistants and models just swooned and giggled together as they gave him appraising looks. Aleksi would likely be faced with one angry Kale when they got back to the hotel. Hell, it might be worth it. Kale was hot when he was calm but Aleksi imagined Kale was stunning when he was angry.

A bell sounded and someone with a clipboard shouted they had five minutes before the show began. Everyone went back to his or her tasks, rushing to get it all finished on time.

Aleksi waited until Kale's gaze met his in the mirror and Aleksi mouthed 'sorry'.

The angry spark didn't disappear, but it lessened, and Kale nodded slightly.

Not forgiven but at least able to sleep without one eye open tonight, Aleksi turned his attention back to their surroundings. There were models and designers everywhere, models trying to breathe in ridiculously tight clothes and somehow wedge their feet into shoes three sizes too small with heels taller than the length of their forearms.

Several models walked past him, looking neither male nor female. Another came past with what looked like a birdcage on her head, followed by a designer who appeared to wearing a coat made from hair.

This is a strange, strange world.

* * * *

Camera flashes went off everywhere. Aleksi stood next to the raised stage and runway that ran the length of the large temporary event room. He'd argued with the head of security until finally he'd had to show his Shifter Protection Specialist, Inc. identification. The fact that the man recognized it straight away told Aleksi their reputation in the industry was solid. Scott would be thrilled when he told him.

After that, Aleksi had had his choice of position and the security team was told to report anything strange — or whatever passed as strange for the fashion world.

The last few models on the schedule were stomping down the runway. Kale would be up again next, closing the show with a bang, according to the creative director's notes. Even the security guy in charge looked impressed that he'd managed to get his hands on a copy of it. Aleksi didn't tell him that he'd taken advantage of the man screaming at assistants to use powder-blue eye shadow instead of duck-egg blue. He'd snatched the guy's clipboard, taken a photo of the information then returned it before the irate director could turn back around.

All he'd had to do then was fire it off to the printer he'd spotted earlier.

The spectators were dressed almost as weirdly as the models. He counted seventeen fake accents in the front row alone. No one appeared to want to be who themselves, preferring to put on an act for those around them.

Unfortunately, that meant Aleksi had to figure out whether they were hiding something because they were fake idiots or whether someone there posed a credible threat to Kale.

No matter what the police said, Aleksi wasn't convinced Not-Barry had given up.

The two models came off the runway after completing their walks and ran behind the curtain to get ready for the next fashion house to take over the show.

He scanned the crowd again, watching people's hands. The audience fell silent and the lights dimmed until just one spotlight remained. Aleksi gasped, speechless, when Kale stepped into the circle of white light. His lover wore a sheer sheet of fabric draped over his head and body. The only other thing Kale had on was a pair of white skintight pants with what looked like safety pins running down the outside legs. The sheer sheet glittered in the intense beam of the spotlight. Wind machines erupted from the stage floor at the end of the runway. The burst of air forced the sheet taught against Kale's front, flapping and waving behind him like silver flames. Kale began his walk, pushing against the fabric, as the wind got stronger the closer he got.

Aleksi stood mesmerized.

Kale looks…magical.

Almost having to rip his eyes away from the beautiful sight, Aleksi focused on the crowd again. They were just as enamored, some open-mouthed and drooling, others obviously short of breath. Aleksi was doing both.

By the time Kale hit his stride, Aleksi was hard as stone and struggling to concentrate on the people in the audience.

Kale was in his element as he reached the end of the runway and nailed his pose.

The wind machines were on almost full power now, pushing the fabric against him like a second skin. All eyes and attention were on him. No one was talking to his or her neighbor or even texting.

As a model, the best you could hope for was having people remember you after you left the room. Right now, he was eclipsing that. Everyone here would remember this show closer. Men rarely closed a designer's show. It was a job usually reserved for whatever girl or woman the press was talking about.

But not this time. This show was *his*.

Kale paused for another minute at the end, doing a small back bend with his arms wide behind him and leaned forward at the ankles so it looked as if the wind were keeping him standing. Cameras flashed in all directions and he smiled. It was like being outside and looking at the stars. Except this time, he got to be one of them.

He did a three count and straightened before turning and letting the draped fabric fly off him and into the hands of a waiting assistant. It was very theatrical but he could honestly say this was his favorite show yet. Hopefully he'd get to work with the designer or creative director again. Their ideas were original, which was surprisingly rare.

On his walk back, Kale let his hips swing a little, adding just a hint more sexuality to his body language. He daren't even look at Aleksi again as he approached the end of the stage. If he did, there would be nowhere to hide his erection in the white pants. He'd probably bust a pin. The heat emanating from the shifter when Kale had stepped into the light had been enough to get him excited and it had given him the confidence to put on a show. The design was a nod to the fashion house's past, bringing it into the present and adapting it to become a statement piece for modern style.

There were only a few more steps and Kale could change and go find Aleksi. The hotel was a twenty-minute drive. But Kale was hoping that if he could talk the creative director into letting him borrow the pants for another half hour. Then maybe he could convince Aleksi to sneak into one of the meeting rooms out back. No one would be using them while the show was on.

As he stopped to do his last pose, a little look over his shoulder and give the crowd a cheeky wink, something caught his eye. He turned to his left in time to see a man launch himself at the stage.

Kale leaped back but managed to stay upright. He couldn't let the audience see how terrified he was. Aleksi would keep him safe. He was one hundred percent sure of that. Kale just had protect himself until Aleksi reached him.

The man scrambled up onto the stage before Aleksi or the security team could get to him and Kale. The high from the walk drained away and Kale sidestepped as the guy made to lunge at him, taking something shiny out of his pocket and wielding it like a knife. His shifter bodyguard jumped onto the stage and landed with the feline grace that seemed to come naturally to him. Aleksi quickly grabbed the man and pushed him off the stage and into the waiting hands of three security guys.

Thank God.

Kale stood rooted to the spot. Everyone was silent and even the runway music had cut out. The spotlight had dimmed as the other lights in the room had come back on. Everyone now looked at him for a different reason now and he wasn't in control.

"It's okay. It's not him, just someone who has had too much to drink. Finish your walk, make them remember that instead," Aleksi whispered it in his ear.

Aleksi kissed him on the cheek. With a push from the shifter, Kale found himself turned around, facing the opposite end of the runway, the way he'd come.

He took a deep breath and forced himself to calm down. This was *his* runway. *He* was closing the show and damn anyone who wanted to take that from him.

Lifting his chin, Kale squared his shoulders and strode halfway up the runway, striking a stronger, less delicate pose than before and spun around. The hint of sexuality from before turned into full-on temptation as he lengthened his strides and rolled his hips in a way that promised sin with his new stamping walk. This wasn't his usual nice, sweet, good-boy walk. It was a pissed-off, confident strut and he fastened his gaze on Aleksi, prowling toward his man who had moved just behind the curtains to the stage entrance, waiting for him. He hoped the message was clear that he was coming for Aleksi.

By the time he got to the curtain this time, he threw a full, heat-filled grin at the audience.

The designer and director ran up to him as soon as he entered the backstage area, full of apologies and praise. "My word, you were wonderful. So alive and exciting. Innocent one minute and sinful the next. You are a delight." The designer kissed his cheeks twice each and waved a hand at Kale's outfit. "You must keep these. I insist."

Kale wasn't going to argue with that. "Thank you. I am sorry your show got ruined."

"Ha! You made the show even better. Half of that lot out there thinks it was all part of the act. I didn't know you had it in you, Kale. Don't be surprised if your agent gets flooded with offers. Where is he, anyway? Your brother usually attends the fashion-week shows to mingle."

"He's probably busy," Kale supplied. His brother had texted him earlier saying he wouldn't make it. It wasn't unusual for Caleb to be caught up in some deal or another, or be on a date with the latest pretty actress trying to make it big. His brother was quite the Casanova in the press. What the journalists didn't know was that Caleb didn't sleep with the actresses he took out on dates. He only introduced them to the right people to give them a foot in the door. Some had gone on to sign Hollywood blockbuster roles.

"No rest for the wicked. And you simply *must* do my next show at Bryant Park." The designer didn't wait for Kale's answer, just ran off chasing after a model who was trying to stuff her designer dress and what looked like half the makeup table into her purse.

"I guess I'll tell Caleb to expect your call," he said lamely, a little overwhelmed. He'd thought the show had been a disaster because of the drunk. It was why he hadn't held back on his last walk. In his mind, he'd had nothing to lose so thought he might as well go out with a bang.

"You must tell him to call me," the creative director crooned.

Kale nodded but he could tell he'd already lost the man's attention when he ran in the opposite direction, talking into the headset to someone named Tyra about her girls needing to be on set in three seconds or they were cut.

Kale just blinked and looked up at Aleksi beside him, blinking again when he couldn't think of anything to say.

The shifter was surveying the room, watching everything that was going on, but he didn't tense, so Kale didn't think anything was wrong. "I think I have a headache."

"Well there goes my plan of a quickie in the meeting room."

Aleksi growled and glared down at him. Kale was beginning to recognize and interpret the shifter's growls. This one was either 'don't speak to me about not eating sugar' or 'I really want to touch you but I need to keep you safe'.

Kale was almost certain that Aleksi didn't care whether he ate sugar or not right now. Kale could practically feel the heat coming off the sex-on-a-stick shifter. Aleksi's bulging arms stretching the almost transparent black material of his T-shirt caught Kale's eye and the muscles jumped as he stared at them. He licked his lips. What he wouldn't give right now to bite them.

"Come on. Let's get back to the hotel where you can do as many safety checks as you want then we can explore what wonderful things I can do with my mouth." He stretched up on tiptoes and kissed Aleksi soundly on the lips. He didn't have to translate the next growl. He grinned as he backed away.

* * * *

As they exited the hotel elevator, Kale hung back a few seconds until Aleksi reached for his hand to tell him it was safe. Kale knocked on the door as they were going past Caleb's room. There was no answer, so his brother must still be out. Kale pulled out his phone to check for missed calls and sure enough, there was a missed call and a text message an hour old from Caleb.

I got invited to an after party for that new action movie with what's his name. Don't wait up. See you in the morning.

Kale quickly typed back a message.

Okay. Have fun and relax for once. Show went great. Expect a flood of designers after my body. ☺

His phone buzzed with a reply from his brother.

Will do.

Kale shrugged at the short text. Caleb must really be having fun nag to not for details. It would do his big brother good to let loose. Mr. Stuffy Shirt aka Caleb might even get laid if he took off the tie and had a few drinks.

The last relationship Caleb was in had ended badly after the woman had tried to climb into bed with Kale, who still felt guilty about it, thinking there might have been a way to prevent the brokenhearted look on his brother's face when Kale had told him. That had been two years ago and no one had managed to get past his brother's walls since.

Come to think of it, the anniversary of that debacle was coming up soon. It might even have been tonight. *Damn, I should really get an actual calendar instead of an event schedule.* This was another thing he needed to change. He'd become entirely too self-absorbed and the world around him was passing him by.

Aleksi squeezed his hand gently, getting his attention. "Let's not linger here. You can call Caleb from your room."

Kale shook his head and continued walking down the corridor until they reached his room. "No, I'll leave him alone. He's probably turned his phone off now for the night anyway so he can have some peace and quiet."

"He did seem a bit tired and weary in Scott's office."

"I know. I worry about him, but he insists he doesn't need a break."

"Perhaps after we catch Not-Barry, you can both stay at my house in the woods for a while."

Aleksi was scanning the area, but Kale could see the shifter was nervous about making the offer. It set a precedent for making plans past Aleksi protecting him.

However, Kale's heart melted at the invitation. He knew Aleksi never let anyone in his house but his family, the people he worked with—it was his sanctuary. To offer it to Kale and his brother said more about how Aleksi felt about their relationship than either of them were ready to admit. Even though Kale wanted to take a step back from the feelings, it didn't sit right with him to leave Aleksi hanging out there on his own.

"That is very sweet. Perhaps we can put him in the room at the other end of the hall, though. I'd want us to be *loud* when I can have you all to myself without a psycho lurking somewhere."

Kale opened the door and watched as Aleksi entered and gave the room a onceover then checked the closet and bathroom. After entering his room, Kale closed the door behind him, waiting to see what the shifter would do. The anticipation fed the tension in the air and he had to wipe his palms on his pants.

"Loud. *How* loud?" Aleksi stalked toward him, totally focused on him now that the room was deemed to be safe. Kale let the shifter crowd him up against the door, laughing as the man swooped in to kiss his neck and smell his hair.

"You always smell so good," Aleksi said with a growl.

Kale grabbed Aleksi's face and brought him down close enough to kiss him. The size difference between them made Kale feel dainty but also amazingly powerful when Aleksi let him lead, even if it was for a few minutes before the cat took control again.

Aleksi took hold of his ass and lifted him. Kale squeaked and slapped his hands on Aleksi's shoulders to keep his balance. When they were the same height, Aleksi pinned him to the door with his heavy body.

He nibbled on Aleksi's bottom lip and tried to rip the shifter's shirt off, but the buttons were stubborn little buggers and stayed where they were, stopping Kale from getting at all of Aleksi's hard muscles and soft chest hair.

Aleksi's erection pressed against Kale's and Kale wrapped his legs around the shifter's waist to press closer. "Shirt off."

Kale moaned when Aleksi leaned back, shoving their fabric-covered cocks together, and ripped the shirt he was wearing apart at the seams. He threw it over his shoulder. Kale about came on the spot at the view of Aleksi's steel-hard chest. Aleksi unzipped Kale's coat and Kale tugged his arms free before throwing that aside too.

"Here or bed?" Aleksi's question penetrated his lust-filled mind.

There was no way Kale was letting the shifter go long enough to go over to the bed.

Kale dragged his mouth away from kissing him and play biting his way across Aleksi's collarbone. "Here."

Aleksi took him at his word and wedged a hand between them to undo Kale's pants. A part of Kale was disappointed he hadn't worn the pants from the show, but they weren't made for sitting in a car or being thrown against a door and debauched while carrying a hard-on solid enough to ram a hole through the wood. They were, however, made to open at all the seams. Kale knew he'd definitely be putting them on later.

He had to lower his feet in order to step out of his pants and, when he was free of them, he kicked the offending fabric away, knocking over a lamp. Kale didn't care. He'd get reception to charge his room for it. Right now, he had a more pressing engagement with the tasty cock hiding inside Aleksi's pants.

Kale attacked the belt and fly keeping him from the massive cock he was dying to taste. They had done all kinds of rubbing and stroking at Aleksi's house and had even jerked each other off in several imaginative ways in Paris, including on the balcony, then had been ticketed by the French police for it. He was putting that damn ticket in a frame when he got home. It was the wildest thing he'd ever done. It had been the early hours of the morning and their third-floor room had overlooked a party boat on the river. Aleksi had dragged him out there after the music had changed from some weird techno mix to old-school rock anthems. After leaning precariously over the iron filigree fencing to check that no one was watching them, of course.

When the shifter had him naked on the balcony and dancing to *Addicted to Love* and *White Wedding*, Kale had gone along with it a bit apprehensively. But once Aleksi had kissed him, all that had gone away. Before Kale's brain had caught up with him, the shifter had been playing his body like a finely tuned instrument. He'd ended up coming to *Livin' on a Prayer* and hotel security banging on the door. Talk about a surreal experience. It was safe to say that Kale wouldn't be going back to that particular hotel any time soon.

He refocused on his task when the damn stubborn zipper released. He stole one more kiss before he sank to his knees and swallowed as much of Aleksi's monster cock as he could.

With something this big, he had to start slowly, but his own arousal was making patience impossible. He growled in frustration as he tried to take more of

Aleksi in his mouth, only to have to back off when his gag reflex kicked in.

"Slow down, kit."

Aleksi had started calling him kit when they were doing anything sexual. Kale had a feeling it was short for kitten or something equally ridiculous, but he didn't want to ask in case it stopped the shifter from doing it anymore. No one had called him by an endearment. It felt nice.

Kale tried again to take Aleksi all the way inside his mouth, but Aleksi was too big. The shifter batted his hands away when Kale tried to fist the shaft of his large cock instead.

"Open," Aleksi instructed, looking down at him with hooded eyes.

Opening his mouth, Kale sat back on his knees and waited. He didn't have to wait long, as Aleksi spread his feet apart, bringing his body lower, then proceeded to feed Kale his massive dick.

The shifter never pushed too hard or too much. Kale sighed at the sensation of Aleksi filling his mouth. He could feel the large head at the back of his tongue and he managed to relax enough to let it pass his gagging point and prod the back of his throat.

They stayed like that for a minute as he got used to breathing calmly and evenly though his nose. Aleksi stilled and Kale couldn't begin to imagine having that much control when he was as aroused as he felt Aleksi was. When he was ready for Aleksi to move, he lifted his hand and tapped Aleksi's thigh to get the shifter's attention since the man had closed his eyes and had thrown his head back. It was a great compliment, but Kale wanted something a little more vocal.

Kale gave a thumbs-up sign to say it was okay to move and got busy stroking his fingers over Aleksi's big balls. Even with Aleksi's cock halfway down his throat, he still wasn't close to taking all of his lover, so he concentrated one hand on the man's heavy balls, rolling them gently while moving his other hand up to curl around the rest of Aleksi's considerable erection.

When the shifter didn't move, he glanced up at Aleksi and sent Aleksi another thumbs-up. Aleksi gave a tentative thrust and Kale kept his breathing regular and relaxed.

The next thrust had a little more force behind it and Kale would have smiled if he could have at the surprise and ecstasy on Aleksi's face. He could see how being this big was a problem for prospective lovers when it came to oral sex. But Kale loved to please his sexual partners this way. It bordered on being his kink and Aleksi was exactly what he'd always dreamed about late at night when he had a dry spell.

He had a fleeting thought that he'd never done this without his hook-up wearing a glove but it quickly flittered away when Aleksi started pumping into his mouth.

Though the moves were careful, never going faster than Kale could handle or further than before, Kale noticed Aleksi was beginning to lose control. The shifter fisted his hands at his sides as if he had to stop them from grabbing Kale's head and fucking his face. Now *that* was much closer to the reaction he wanted.

The mix of Aleksi's iron will and the signs of the big shifter letting go was a hell of a turn-on. Kale humped the air in search of any kind of friction and gave a growl of his own when he couldn't find any. The vibration must have set off his lover because Aleksi urgently surged forward, almost—but not quite—

going too far, rubbing his swollen cockhead across Kale's tongue.

Getting the message, Kale started sucking and licking the red cap every time Aleksi pulled out far enough. He had to let go of Aleksi's cock and put his hand on Aleksi's hip instead, digging his fingers into the hard flesh to keep himself steady as Aleksi sped up. The big shifter moved impossibly fast until Kale squeezed the man's heavy balls again, knowing it was a hotspot. Aleksi roared and gave him everything he had, filling Kale's mouth with release.

As he swallowed, Kale massaged Aleksi's balls and kept his gaze on the shifter. He clenched his ass cheeks when Aleksi's eyes flashed to cat. He couldn't wait to see that image with Aleksi buried inside him. The little thrill of danger was enough to make him pant and lick his lips as they dried instantly.

He milked Aleksi through his orgasm and swallowed every bit of the hot liquid until Aleksi withdrew and collapsed to his knees.

His own erection screamed at him to take notice and he jumped on Aleksi, rolling the shifter fully onto his back and straddling him. He grasped himself and squeezed, whining at how desperate he was to come. It only took a few hard strokes to finish himself off and Kale fell forward to cry out into Aleksi's neck, coming over his lover's deliciously hard abs.

They lay like that for a while with Aleksi purring softly. Kale snuggled closer and tried to ignore the carpet burn starting to sting his knees. He'd slap some cream on it later. It was totally worth it.

Thankfully, Aleksi somehow still had enough brainpower to think, because the shifter kissed him on the nose and asked, "Here or bed?"

"Bed," he moaned, not looking forward to the prospect of actually having to move. He should have known better, though.

With a lurch, Aleksi picked him up and stood, then he walked over to the bed and deposited him on it unceremoniously before falling face-first onto the bouncy mattress himself.

They snuggled up together and Kale promised to get something to clean up Aleksi in a minute or two, but the shifter pulled him closer and curled around him.

Chapter Six

Aleksi watched Kale's eyes flutter open as the man woke up. "I'm sorry." The words were out before he could call them back. Aleksi had been awake for what seemed like hours, thinking.

"What?" His lover frowned and scrubbed his eyes as he yawned widely.

Aleksi sighed and lay back. He'd already ruined the morning afterglow so he might as well get it out in the open. He'd spent more than enough time arguing with himself about it. "I should have thought to wear a condom. I'm sorry."

Kale looked wide-awake now, sitting up and leaning over him. Aleksi struggled against the urge to just bite him and claim him so everyone would know Kale was taken.

So much for taking things slow and not jumping in too soon.

"I feel like I've missed a conversation. Were you talking to yourself while I was asleep?"

Aleksi growled at the question. It didn't matter if he had been—it had no relevance here. Kale really needed to grasp the seriousness of the situation. They'd been irresponsible and Aleksi was unnerved by the potential fallout of their moment of insanity. He knew better than to act like a hormone-addled teenager, but the minute he let himself think about Kale's lithe body brushing against his, all sense and reason flew out the window.

"We didn't use a condom when you gave me that earthshaking blow job. I didn't even think to ask and now we may have started the bonding process because my tiger wants me to claim you as my mate."

Kale tried to tempt him in for a kiss and Aleksi felt himself being dragged into the man's orbit before he snapped out of it.

"Stop it."

"*Earthshaking*, huh?" Kale preened under his praise.

Aleksi rolled his eyes. Trust Kale to focus on that. This was a very serious situation and he couldn't think of a way out of it that didn't make him feel truly miserable. Scott could send in another guard and Aleksi could leave and never see Kale again. That way he could get his tiger to accept that a mating bond wasn't going to happen. Or he could stay by Kale's side, following him around like a damn fool puppy and forever be on the brink of mating until the human accepted or rejected him outright. As choices went, they were all rather fucked up.

In complete contrast to the light speed of his thoughts, Aleksi blinked and slowly shook his head incredulously. Didn't the man understand what he'd said?

"That's what you took from everything I just told you?"

Kale held up a finger as if to correct him. "You only said *may*. A mate basically means married for life, right?"

Aleksi huffed at the simplification. It was a hell of a lot more than marriage. For one thing, there was no such thing as divorce with a shifter mate bond. "Yes, with more strings."

"Okay. Let's focus on the things we *know*. I'm clean. And you said before that shifters can't catch those sorts of diseases, that your bodies burn it off or something. So that's one thing off the worry list for not using a condom. I can't get pregnant so that's another one to cross off. As for the mate thing, it's not definite. A shifter I was friendly with a few years back said he slept with a girl in college, who he wanted to mate, but that they separated and he got over the compulsion after a few months. So it's not the end of the world, okay?"

Truthfully, he was both relieved and angry at the calm assessment of their situation. That didn't stop him from narrowing his eyes and hauling Kale closer to him. "How friendly?"

Kale tried to push away but gave up when it was clear Aleksi wasn't budging. "We were friends on the job. I haven't heard from him for over a year."

"Good," Aleksi huffed.

"Jealous much?"

Aleksi growled in answer, not liking how unaffected Kale seemed by all this.

Kale rolled his eyes and petted him, saying, "So we can just use a condom from now on and that should quell the mating compulsion until we figure out where this is going."

"Quell?" The old-fashioned word sounded strange coming from Kale.

"What? I read," Kale defended.

Aleksi ignored the smile tugging at his lips. This was no laughing matter. "I don't think you understand the severity of this. My tiger is set on you. If I'm honest, it has been building since we were at my home and you didn't run from me or my saber." Aleksi stared up at the ceiling and refused to look at Kale. He despised being this vulnerable. He should have known better than to get caught up in the feelings that had crept up on him since walking into Scott's office and agreeing to work with the pretty-boy model. He *did* know better. This wasn't some Hollywood film that would have a happy ending as they ran off into the sunset together. Being distracted could get one or both of them killed.

Kale pulled away and this time Aleksi let the human go.

"Really?"

"Yes," Aleksi admitted. He didn't elaborate.

The bed moved and he heard Kale's footsteps even on the soft, carpeted floor. Aleksi's curiosity got the better of him. He had to see where Kale had gone. Aleksi could lie and say it was because of his bodyguard responsibilities, but that would be a farce, considering he had just slept with his protectee. He was almost certain that he would be asked to leave when the man digested everything he'd said.

Kale was looking out of the widow, giving Aleksi a side profile that made his cock take notice. Kale was stunningly handsome and had a body to die for.

He ignored how irresistible Kale was. That was why he in this trouble to begin with.

"So you're saying, after we agreed to take this slow and not put any expectations on whatever it is, that you now want to mate me?"

"I don't *want* to."

Kale's snapped his head in Aleksi's direction. Aleksi leaped out of bed to try to stop the vicious barbs ready to fly from Kale's tongue. Aleksi slowly approached Kale and tried to find a better way to voice the complicated feelings he was having.

"It's not a conscious decision. To say my cat *wants* you is like saying I *want* to breathe. I like you...and I was hoping that after you didn't need me to protect you anymore that we could date. I know it's too soon to even begin thinking about mating—"

Kale snorted and lifted his hands in the universal sign for *exactly.*

"But I cannot deny that I wish to know you better or that the thought of you with another does not result in my wanting to kill something."

He knew he was reverting to the Russian accent he'd lost over the years living in America. When he was stressed or anxious, he couldn't help it. The formal speech let him claw back some control and composure, even though inside he was anything but calm.

"We haven't even had sex yet!"

His cat didn't like the reminder but he managed to quash the hiss and disguise the noise with a cough. A deadly glare from Kale let him know he hadn't gotten away with it.

Where was all his stoic calm? The few lovers he'd had over the years had labeled him cold and emotionless. Aleksi would trade everything he owned to be that way now. All these feelings and talking about feelings had him ready to peel off his own skin just so he had something else less painful to deal with.

A knot of insecurity tightened in his chest. "Did you feel nothing when we pleased each other? Was this truly casual to you?"

He could see the answer on Kale's face and it was like a knife to the back. No, it was worse. He'd actually had a dagger in his back once and it had hurt less than this.

"So it would not bother you at all if I were to fuck the next person I meet? You wouldn't care if I found a hot blond to take home and fucked him up against the door or if I picked up a stacked brunette and carried her to my bed and gave her as much pleasure as her pert, tight body could stand, satisfying myself thoroughly in the arms and body of another."

Kale flinched with every one of Aleksi's descriptions, but he still didn't say anything.

He'd never really been attracted to women, but Aleksi wanted drive his point home. The mere thought of sleeping with someone other than Kale was excruciating but admitting that wouldn't help him plead his case.

Aleksi narrowed his gaze in on Kale's face, noting the pinch around the man's lips and the frown trying to form between his eyes. He took that as encouragement. It gave him hope he wasn't alone in this mess.

He waited until Kale's gaze met his before continuing and forcing his eyes to change.

Every time he'd climaxed with Kale he hadn't been able to stop the small shift. In hindsight, it should have been a clue for him to take extra precautions. But he'd also noticed how hot it made Kale when he did it and how much he liked it when Aleksi lost control.

"Or your brother. I understand he's straight, but I'm sure I could persuade him to experiment. He is very attractive and I scented his appreciation of my body when I entered the office, just as I did yours. I could..."

Kale shot his hand up as if to ward off his words. "Stop! You've made your point. I wouldn't be fine with it."

Secretly, Aleksi breathed a sigh of relief. He'd had nothing after that. He'd played all the cards he could think of. He let his eyes change back to human.

"Fine. We'll give this a go—the dating part, not the irrevocable mating part. And I can't believe I'm saying this...but I want strings." Kale stalked back to the bed, grabbing Aleksi's hand and dragging him along.

Immediately wary and cautious at the sudden surrender, Aleksi sat next to Kale and watched him fuss with his hair that was standing up at all angles.

"Strings?"

"Yes. Monogamy is the main one. Don't you ever make a move on my brother or I'll shave you in tiger form. Cohabitation is another condition."

Ignoring the threat, Aleksi lowered his eyebrows. "You want to move in?" He hadn't lived with anyone since he was a small child and the thought of someone constantly in his space was unsettling.

Kale shook his head. "No. I want to know I *can* one day, if our dating relationship goes well."

Aleksi frowned. This was getting confusing. They'd started with from him trying to convince Kale to agree to some sort of commitment and relationship. Now it looked like the tables had turned.

Aleksi searched for any sign of deceit or anything suspicious—as though Kale was hiding something—but he found nothing. He had no choice. "I agree to both terms." His tiger would accept nothing less.

"Then I guess you're my boyfriend," Kale announced in to the silence of the room, sounding shocked and a little confused.

Aleksi knew the feeling.

* * * *

Aleksi was still trying to figure out whether he'd won the argument when they went down for breakfast. To make matters worse, Kale seemed overly cheerful, as if he was trying to compensate for something and kept giving Aleksi thoughtful glances. The tense atmosphere between them had gotten so bad that both of them had tried to engage the waiter in conversation to break the painful silence, all the while pretending that everything was fine and that they weren't *freaking the fuck out* as Jazz, Robert and Scott's little brother said far too often.

Even his cat was unusually quiet. Aleksi knew it wasn't satisfied with the agreement to date exclusively and explore feelings to see if they were compatible before rushing into a mating. The cat wanted Kale claimed right now.

He'd long since finished his morning fix of tea but he still held the cup until he was certain he looked ridiculous using the piece of tiny china as a shield.

Kale was the first one to address the saber-tooth tiger in the room.

"So, this is awkward."

"Yes, it is." Aleksi sighed and gave up the pretense that he was still drinking. He placed the cup down with a soft clink as it rattle on the saucer. "I didn't want to ruin the easy friendship we had before, but unfortunately I cannot change the circumstances." His Russian was showing again.

Kale became very quiet and tense.

Aleksi couldn't explain why. He surveyed the hotel breakfast lounge but nothing seemed amiss and his cat didn't sense any danger or threats. The other guests were too involved with themselves or their companions to pay them any mind. "What is it?"

"You would change it." The light, seductive quality to Kale's voice that Aleksi had come to enjoy was gone. It could have been a robot speaking

What was Kale talking about? "I don't understand."

Kale fiddled with the used cutlery on the dirty plate the waiter had yet to take away. The man was clearly upset about something.

"You said that you couldn't change the circumstances. So, you'd rather your tiger be set on having someone else," Kale concluded in that same toneless voice that made Aleksi want to hit things. Why had his cat decided they should suddenly be in a relationship? Aleksi was no good at navigating the unfamiliar pitfalls. Apart from his family at the company and his protectee, he had very little contact with people — he didn't like them.

"I—"

Kale jumped up from the table before Aleksi could finish his thought.

"I need to check on Caleb. He probably has a killer hangover." Kale took off, leaving Aleksi struggling to get out from the small table and follow his protectee without knocking everything over. He still wasn't sure exactly what had happened to break the awkward, but friendly, truce between them.

The confusing man entered the elevator as soon as it opened, despite Aleksi's numerous warnings about doing such things. If not for his shifter speed, Aleksi doubted he would have made the elevator before the doors closed. Thankfully his brain caught up with his mouth before he could say anything to make the situation worse.

As the car rode up through the floor levels, Aleksi replayed the conversation at the table in his head. When he figured out what he'd said to set Kale off, he could have kicked himself at his stupidity. Perhaps shifters weren't the superior species.

Despite Kale being a successful model and in demand from designers and fans alike, there was an insecurity there. Aleksi had noticed underneath Kale's public face the man believed that no one could really want him for anything other than his body or take him seriously.

By the time they reached Caleb's room, Kale was working up a bad mood. When he was starting to think that maybe, just maybe, someone was interested in him and not his body, that a man like Aleksi could want something solid with him, reality came over to kick him in the nuts. Then the bitch backed over him with a car to be sure he knew his place and not to expect anything more.

On the surface, what Aleksi said might have been innocent but the shifter had been quite vocal upstairs that morning about not wanting to mate with Kale. At first, it had freaked him out. Commitment and Kale didn't exactly go hand in hand.

After the initial shock had worn off, there had been the beginning of something stirring in his chest that he now refused to look at or think about. He should have known better than to become emotionally invested. It only led to getting hurt.

He shook his head in disappointment and knocked on his brother's door. Frowning, he knocked again when there was no answer and checked his watch. Caleb was usually an early riser, even when he was suffering the morning-after effects of the night before. Caleb's cheeriness in the morning had caused many an argument between them while Kale had tried to sleep the day away in the past.

"Perhaps Mr. Andrews is still asleep. You did say he was having a good night last night," Aleksi offered, no doubt trying to be helpful but only succeeding in pissing Kale off more.

"Caleb doesn't do sleeping in—the same way I don't do getting up with the sun." His response might have been a bit more clipped than what was called for, but he couldn't help the frosty attitude. The ice persona was taking over.

This always happened—at least it had when he was younger. Caleb and he had had another brother, Garrick. Garrick had been his older brother by seven years, Caleb's by six, and a through-and-through bad boy. But he'd always made time for them, whether it was picking them up from school or teaching them how to drive, despite the fact that they were years too young to actually do it legally.

One day Garrick didn't come home. It had been Kale's thirteenth birthday and they'd waited hours for Garrick to get back to base, returning from some classified operation. Garrick had signed up for the Army when he was eighteen and had been head hunted by a new team under the Marine Corps. Kale remembered everything about the day his brother's teammate came over to them, his uniform splattered in red, something silver dangling from his hands.

"We were ambushed. I'm so unbelievably sorry for your loss," the man had said. Since then, Kale, commitment and emotions didn't mix. The only person he let himself love was Caleb. Everyone else was a passing acquaintance or a distraction. He didn't even have friends, just people he worked with.

So he couldn't blame Aleksi for not wanting to bind himself to Kale for the rest of his life. Hell, Kale wouldn't want to either. He'd gotten caught up in the moment and let his guard down around the shifter.

It would not happen again.

Aleksi pushed him out of the way and cocked his head, obviously listening for something. Kale raised his eyebrows when the shifter's face turned slightly pink.

Curious, Kale shoved Aleksi and pressed his ear to the door. He snapped back when he heard a guttural moan and recognized the telltale sound of furniture hitting a wall. Even after he'd pulled away from the door, Kale could hear a scream and someone calling for God. He could have lived a long and happy life having never heard his brother having sex or making someone cry for Jesus. "Holy shit. Is there such a thing as ear bleach? Because I need some."

"Your brother sounds preoccupied. We can call back later, if you want to." Again, there was a slight note of apology in the shifter's voice.

Kale grit his teeth and ignored it. "Fine. I'll go back to my room to change, then I want to see the sights. I've never been here for a stopover longer than a few hours before."

"Sounds good. Why can't you go in what you're wearing?"

"These are my clothes. I'm paid to wear designer clothes and jewelry in public."

"Oh." Kale didn't have to ask what Aleksi thought of that. People not in the business didn't understand

and Kale wasn't going to explain it. He could tell it was another mark against him.

Well, screw Aleksi and his disappointed glances. Kale earned more in a year than most models made in ten. He and Caleb had worked damn hard to make it that way. The more he made, the more they could give to the veterans' charities. At a rough estimate, they had managed to give over two million dollars to rehabilitation, grieving spouses, children of brave people who served, scholarships and guide dogs for injured soldiers, Marines, SEALS and many more—all in Garrick's name.

Aleksi didn't know him and apparently he didn't want to.

Kale stomped down the corridor to his room, not caring if he looked ridiculous. All of his attitude fled, smothered by a wave of fear when he saw the door standing ajar. He stopped dead and didn't argue when Aleksi pushed him flat to the wall.

The big shifter pressed against him, leaving no part of Kale exposed and despite his issues with Aleksi, he did trust the man implicitly when it came to his safety.

Aleksi got his attention by producing a gun from behind his back and leaning down to press his lips to Kale's ear. "I can't hear or smell anyone inside. But we know that Not-Barry has access to scent blockers. I need you to get behind me when I move and stick to me like a second skin. We're going to go backward but move fast."

"I need to tell Caleb—"

"When you're safe," Aleksi interrupted, leaving no room for negotiation.

Before Kale could argue, Aleksi stepped away from him and quickly whipped him around with a strong arm so that he faced Aleksi's back. He did as he was told and clung to the shifter's body, his fingers in the man's belt loops, and moved when Aleksi moved.

Aleksi raised the gun and turned them so that they were facing his hotel room. Just as Aleksi warned, they moved fast and if he hadn't been holding on to Aleksi, he would have fallen on his ass more than once by the time they entered the elevator. Aleksi didn't put the weapon down when they were in the secure metal box, only tensed as if ready for anything and listening to everything.

If Kale wasn't angry and scared right then, he would have totally jumped the hot shifter and demanded Aleksi take him in the elevator. Kale snorted to himself. It sounded dirtier than he'd meant it to.

Chapter Seven

The elevator dinged to signal its arrival on the ground floor and Kale found himself once again pushed flat against the metal wall as the door opened. Loud voices shattered the small amount of calm he'd managed to force into himself. "*Polizia*! Come out slowly with your hands in the air," a man with a thick Italian accent called out.

"Fuck."

Aleksi cursing couldn't be a good thing.

Kale stayed quiet and didn't move when Aleksi pushed him in closer until the wall bar dug into his back and Aleksi shouted back a fluent torrent of Italian. He wasn't even surprised that Aleksi knew Italian. The shifter seemed full of hidden talents

"I repeat. Come out slowly and put your weapon on the ground."

"And I repeat. I cannot do that, I'm protecting my charge, model Kale Andrews. I am a close-protection specialist working with Shifter Protection Specialists, Inc. I cannot let my protectee out until I know he will be safe. His room has been broken into. Room four sixty-three."

Kale flinched when there was a wave of aggressive Italian bellowed from outside when Aleksi said who he worked for. He could imagine the panic going through the local police. They wouldn't know what kind of shifter Aleksi was, but they would know he was dangerous, just from the sheer size of him as a human. The last thing he needed was for one of the police to get trigger happy.

Aleksi switched back to Italian and Kale had no idea what was exchanged but they seemed to have reached an understanding. The shifter relaxed slightly and pulled back enough that Kale was finally able to take a full intake of breath.

"Stay close to me and don't make any sudden movements," Aleksi cautioned before slowly taking Kale's hand and leading him out of the elevator.

He didn't know what he was expecting, but it wasn't for the police to charge suddenly at them, weapons raised as they surrounded him and Aleksi.

Several of the police tried to snatch him, grabbing at his arms harshly, making him yelp in surprise and pain. He would definitely have bruises. Aleksi threw his head back and roared, an angry sound that Kale was glad wasn't aimed in his direction.

"Aleksi!"

Another uniformed police officer jumped Aleksi from behind, smacking a metal police baton over Aleksi's head when Aleksi tried to free Kale.

Kale jerked against the painful hold. "No!"

Aleksi went down hard, falling to his knees as Kale struggled to get to his bodyguard. Kale yanked against the hold until the police officers had to either let him go or break his arm. Thankfully they chose to let him go, yelling something at him in Italian. He leaned down in front of Aleksi and put his hands on the man's cheeks, lifting his face so that he could see the damage.

A nasty cut on the side of Aleksi's head bled so much that it was turning his blond hair red as well as dripping on the floor. But while that was a concern, it wasn't the most pressing issue. Aleksi's eyes had gone completely cat and Kale shivered at the anger in them. This was nothing like when the shifter's eyes changed with passion. There was no humanity in Aleksi's eyes right then, only pissed-off saber-tooth tiger.

Kale spun around and tried to keep himself between Aleksi and the police. Aleksi was on his feet now and trying to dodge around Kale, but he couldn't seem to do it without shoving Kale out of the way. He knew neither Aleksi nor his tiger would risk hurting him if they viewed him as their mate or potential mate. He just had to keep Aleksi from getting to the police until his lover was back in his right mind. The last thing he wanted was for Aleksi to cause an international incident and end up in jail. There were different laws here regarding shifters and Kale wasn't sure he'd be able to get Aleksi out if he was imprisoned.

"Stop! *Basta, basta!*"

The police officer who was shouting came toward them. Aleksi growled low and dangerously, using Kale's distraction to slip around in front of him. But the shifter stayed with him when he yelped as one of the grabbers tried for him again and missed, hitting his arm where they'd bruised him. Aleksi hissed at them and shielded Kale with his big body. It was kind of hot and Kale ducked his head as his face heated when Aleksi sniffed the air and turned to look at him.

Getting turned on at the wrong time was becoming a too-often occurrence for his liking. Kale really needed to sort his inappropriate attraction to Aleksi under control whenever his lover became all growly and protective.

Rapid Italian came from both the new officer and the puffed-up officer who was clearly in charge of this little gathering. The new one, who was tall and thin with shiny black hair, pointed to Aleksi frantically, waving his hand at the police officers. The one in charge went from purple with anger to ashen gray, glancing at Kale and Aleksi as the new officer continued to berate him.

Aleksi continued growling and paced back and forth in front of Kale like an angry tiger stalking prey that it couldn't reach. Kale didn't think Aleksi would hesitate to pounce on the officers if an opportunity presented itself where Kale would be safe. He wasn't sure how he felt about it, though. This was the first time he'd seen Aleksi's cat without any of his lover's control. It didn't help much to know he was the only safe person here.

Finally, the yelling stopped and the police left, all looking shame-faced. The new guy had obviously ripped them a new one. If the police officer hadn't been trying to drag them off a few minutes ago, Kale would have found it funny.

"Gio, it's nice to see you again, old friend. I see your knack for showing up at the right time hasn't left you," Aleksi greeted warmly. He'd come back to himself when he'd heard the familiar—yet irate—voice of his friend.

Aleksi was a mix between touched beyond words that Kale had protected him from himself and angry that the man had put himself in harm's way.

The blow to the head with the police baton had caught him by surprise and his tiger had taken over while he'd recovered and healed the damage to his skull. If he had been human, the strike would have killed him. As it was, he had a killer headache but not much damage apart from to his pride. He should be the one protecting Kale, not the other way around.

Gio came closer and flung his arms wide. Aleksi let the dark-haired man pull him into a hug then kissed his cheeks, but he couldn't help flicking his gaze toward Kale. If looks could kill, Gio would be in the ground. He never thought he'd be so happy to see Kale throwing a death glare in his direction.

Despite everything, Kale did care, did want him.

"It has been a long time, tiger," Gio teased him in Italian. The man stepped back, smiling, and shot a glance in Kale's direction.

His lover was now pointedly ignoring them, picking at some imaginary dirt from under his fingernails. Aleksi's cat liked that Kale felt possessive.

"What trouble have you gotten yourself into this time? You are like a magnet for it. It is a wonder you are still standing," Gio retorted with a sly glance at Kale.

"Now, we *both* know the last time we were in trouble with that car bomb it was entirely *your* fault," Aleksi pointed out with a grin. They had switched back to English and he noticed out of the corner of his eye that Kale was unobtrusively trying to listen in on their conversation.

"We will have to agree to disagree there, my friend. Now, tell me about this tip that was sent into the station. An armed rogue shifter has taken a hostage, along with your photo."

Aleksi frowned at the information. "A tip? When was this?"

Gio shrugged. "Around one hour ago. The runts picked the tip up and ran — without getting clearance from their boss, by the way. My superior spotted the photo on one of their desks after they'd left." Runts were what he and Gio called officers new to the force who wanted to make a name for themselves. Runts had been one of the biggest obstacles when he and Gio had been protecting the Italian president.

Aleksi knew Gio was suspicious of what was going on inside his head. Gio would no doubt recognize the look in his face. They'd spent months together working protection detail together after all.

"What are you thinking?"

Kale's question caught him off guard. "How would anyone know I would have my gun out and was transporting you down in the lift at precisely this time when we should have been in your room? Unless..."

"Unless they had planned it that way and the open door to my room was a set-up." Kale caught on to what he was getting at and frowned.

Nodding, Aleksi stepped closer to Kale. Neither the human part of him nor the tiger liked the fact that they'd been played. Another thought struck him and he turned back to the tall Italian. "Gio, where would Kale have been taken if the runts had succeeded in grabbing him?"

Gio frowned as if he couldn't follow Aleksi's train of thought. "To be processed at the station until it was confirmed he was a victim and given his statement, signed paperwork and the like."

He turned to his friend. "Gio, I need you to call whoever is running front of house at the station and tell them to see if there is anyone waiting around in the background, looking expectant or seeming nervous or excited."

Calling on his phone instead of the radio to prevent anyone from overhearing the conversation, Gio did as he asked. When his friend's gaze shot to his, Aleksi had his answer even without listening in on the conversation. "Tell them not to let him leave. The man is wanted for several murders in the US, including two police officers."

Kale hugged close to Aleksi's side and he glanced down to see the man was trying to phone someone on his cell. From Kale's frustrated grimace, he wasn't getting through. His protectee must be trying to contact his brother. Aleksi put an arm around Kale's shoulders in a brief hug. "Try texting. If he's…busy he might not want to speak to you."

"What do you…? *Oh.*" Kale blushed delightfully again.

Damn. Aleksi couldn't believe how stunning the man was. If he was given even the smallest of chances to keep Kale as his mate, Aleksi was grabbing it with his saber teeth.

Gio was still talking with whoever was at the station but from the furious glower his usually happy and easygoing friend wore, Aleksi could tell it was bad news before Gio even ended the call. Though, the violent stab of the End Call button was a clue too. "The man spooked, grabbed an old lady who was bringing her grandson lunch and used her as a human shield until he got out of the building and ran into a bus load of tourists. My men lost him. I'm sorry, my friend. He's in the wind."

Cursing, Aleksi dragged a hand roughly through is hair. This guy was too slippery.

A hand on his biceps got his attention and he turned to look down at Kale again. "Hey, we'll get him." Kale held up his phone, showing Aleksi the new text and forced a laugh. "Caleb doesn't even know anything has happened. He seems like he's having a great time with his hook-up. He still sounds drunk if his texting is anything to go by."

Aleksi had to smile at that. "Caleb seems like he could use a good way to relax. He's too stiff." Then he realized what he'd said and they both shared a real, if short, laugh.

He sobered and returned his attention to Gio. "I think Kale's room was broken into as part of the ploy to get us down here with me waving my gun around."

After a minute, Gio grimaced with understanding as he obviously put the pieces together. It was odd. Usually he and Gio were on the same wavelength but Kale had figured out what he was thinking long before his friend.

"I will go up and check it out." Gio waited for Aleksi to promise not to cause any more trouble before heading to the elevator, laughing as Aleksi glared at him.

* * * *

Once Gio had cleared the room, Aleksi had grudgingly agreed to let Kale back up there while Gio and a few different police officers kept an eye on the elevators and stairs. Aleksi didn't doubt that this wasn't the last they'd see of Not-Barry.

Aleksi shot into the bathroom when Kale shouted for him, claws out and ready to shred the stalker into little pieces. But he only found Kale standing by the sink, looking horrified.

"I'm sorry, I didn't think. I'm fine," Kale apologized again and Aleksi scented the air to make sure there wasn't any danger before pulling his claws back in and studying his lover.

"Why did you shout?"

"It's nothing," Kale answered quickly.

Kale wouldn't meet his eyes and Aleksi's cat grumbled. He didn't like the fact that there was a wall between them now. Before he'd dropped the M-bomb, everything had been fine — or as fine as it could be with a dangerous stalker trying to abduct Kale.

"Tell me," he encouraged softly.

"He stole my shampoo, my shower gel and my underwear from this morning. Then I saw a shadow through the window and almost had a heart attack. It was only a bird, though." Kale shrugged.

Aleksi scented the overly sweet smell of embarrassment. Aleksi hadn't been expecting that sort of response and it threw him for a moment. "Do you want me to eat it?"

As responses go, that wasn't one of his best, but his tiger felt that it had been a perfectly reasonable offer.

Open-mouthed, Kale stared at him for a minute and Aleksi resisted the urge to run or growl. Stupid responses or growling at the man wasn't likely to make Kale any more inclined to share things with him.

"Umm…no, that's not necessary. Thanks, though."

Aleksi tried to seem nonchalant as he nodded. "Okay, then."

Kale must have seen his discomfort, as the man came closer to Aleksi and put a hand on Aleksi's chest before stretching up and kissing him on the cheek.

Aleksi couldn't remember anyone doing that before and he felt his heart skip just a little faster.

Stepping back quickly, Kale bit his bottom lip as if he were as affected as Aleksi by the simple contact.

Aleksi awkwardly gave Kale a kiss on the lips—a light one simply because he couldn't resist. "I think it would be best if you moved hotels until we leave Milan."

"I want to pack my stuff and get out. I'll change our flight for tonight instead of tomorrow. I want out of here," Kale announced with a shudder.

Aleksi couldn't blame him one bit. Somehow stealing shower gel, shampoo and underwear made the crazy would-be kidnapper even creepier.

* * * *

The earliest flight back home with three seats available on it was at midnight. Hours away. So Aleksi came up with the plan that they not check out of this hotel but also book a night in the hotel next door under a different name. He, Kale and Caleb would stay in the second hotel and no one else would be any the wiser. Not-Barry should think they either were in the same room as before or had gone to one far away from it until they could get a flight out of Italy.

It was a game of cat and mouse. Aleksi had an unparalleled advantage at cat and mouse—he was the biggest damn cat there was.

He didn't want to be caught in the same situation again, so Aleksi insisted they get rooms on the first floor. There were more escape routes available and less opportunity for Not-Barry to set a trap at every one.

Caleb had reluctantly agreed to say goodbye to his hook-up when Kale told him what was going on and was packing before coming over to join them in the new hotel. Aleksi watched through the small slit in the curtains, observing people coming in and out of the building.

"How did Gio know you were in trouble, anyway? Your friend was *very* happy to see you." Kale's question wasn't so much about what had caught his interest as it was the way he'd said it. Was Kale jealous?

"I protected the previous Italian president a few years ago when there were assassination attempts against him. The older, higher-up police remember me. These new, young, arrogant ones just want to make a name for themselves and make bids for promotions. Good luck to them with that now. I haven't seen Gio since the protection detail ended."

Aleksi wondered if he should tell Kale that he and Gio had slept together once after the assignment was over, before he'd had to return to the States. It was long in the past and he knew it had meant nothing more than lust to both he and the Italian. They hadn't had the talk about previous lovers yet and it was still uncertain as to whether Kale wanted to take it further between them.

"Oh. Were you two…close?"

"We were friends, as I said. But if you're asking if we had sex then yes, before I returned home we slept together, once." He knew he sounded defensive, but he couldn't stop himself. Now that he'd found Kale, his tiger disliked that he had been with anyone else and he certainly didn't want to think about his mate sleeping with anyone else either.

"We could have stayed if you'd wanted to. You two could have caught up. *Gio* certainly wanted to, judging by how he kept touching you...and how you *let* him."

There was definitely something dangerous in Kale's tone, so Aleksi decided to be brutally honest. "Kale, despite the fact that we've agreed to be exclusive while we court each other—and I keep my word—I feel I must point out that I have already slept with Gio and if me or my tiger wanted him for more than a night, we wouldn't be with you now."

Aggravating the sensitive situation probably wasn't the best course of action. But his temper had been pricked.

He watched Kale do a good impression of a fish before he continued, "Since I've met you, I have not looked at another that way. My tiger is set on you and even though my human half is scared, the events today confirmed it. You are brave and smart and you tried to protect me when I was vulnerable. I would very much like to call you my mate." By the end of his confession, he was almost shouting and he threw his hands in the air at himself. He couldn't even do that bit right. What hope did he have of convincing the human to be his mate?

* * * *

Kale lay on the bed, staring up at the white ceiling, replaying Aleksi's words over in his head. No one had ever called him brave or smart before. They certainly hadn't shouted it at him either. He couldn't say it hadn't been endearing, though.

Aleksi had given him space and after an hour of staring at the ceiling, Kale was still no closer to figuring out how he felt about the whole thing.

The ice walls he'd erected around himself had all but shattered when he'd seen the runt strike Aleksi with the baton. Since then, he'd just been confused and more than a little jealous of the Italian police officer who'd swanned in and tried to make a claim on Aleksi as if he had a right to do so.

He was definitely scared, but there was also something inside pushing him to take a chance on Aleksi, telling him that the shifter would never leave him as his brother had or stop loving him as his parents had.

Normally, when he needed to talk something out, Caleb would poke at him and wheedle until he gave in and Kale told his brother everything, but Caleb had been called into a phone meeting about their investments. Kale had never understood the business side of things. Caleb thrived on it, so Kale left him to it—even if it did sometimes drive him mad that his brother was constantly working. Kale just showed up and did the photo shoots, strutted down the runway, delivered his lines in advertisements, charmed the interviewers and schmoozed the people in charge.

He knew he couldn't hide out here indefinitely, but he didn't really want to go and face Aleksi yet either. It wasn't fair to keep jerking the shifter around. Mating was a serious thing and essentially altered Aleksi's life forever, no matter what Kale decided.

As that thought left him, Kale frowned. He'd been thinking about how it affected him and how he didn't know what to do and somehow he'd forgotten that he wasn't the only one in this situation. Aleksi had been reluctant to admit the possibility that they could be mates and had seemed to be even more reluctant to tell Kale how he felt or what he wanted. And yet...Aleksi had taken the leap and declared his interest and intentions, letting Kale have time to himself when it must have hurt when he didn't return the shifter's feelings. Except, Kale wasn't too sure he didn't return those feelings.

Didn't Kale owe it to Aleksi to try?

"Damn it," he sighed, resigned.

Rolling off the bed, he grabbed a packet from his case and shoved it in his pocket. He strode out of the bedroom and into the small sitting area where Aleksi was seated by the window. The shifter turned his way when Kale walked in but quickly put on a guarded expression, his eyes turning cold, but not before Kale saw the crushing sadness and loneliness there.

While he felt awful that he'd put that there, it made his decision easier. Kale didn't stop until he reached Aleksi, then climbed right into the shifter's lap. Aleksi had to either wrap his big arms around him or let him fall on his ass. Kale was relieved when Aleksi chose to catch him.

"What are you doing, Kale?"

"I'm claiming my mate," he said with a grin and a wink before grabbing Aleksi's face and taking the shifter's mouth with a demanding kiss. Aleksi didn't respond at first but Kale coaxed him into the kiss, spearing his tongue out to flick Aleksi's top lip. He groaned with pleasure when the shifter kissed him back and they fought for control.

When they broke apart, they were both breathing heavily and Kale squirmed on Aleksi's lap, feeling the shifter's excitement pressing against his ass.

Kale laughed when he raised a growl from Aleksi. The shifter grabbed his hips and forced him down onto Aleksi's groin to get more friction. The show of strength and the glimpse of Aleksi's not-so-human teeth made him hot enough that he thought his erection might well rip through his pants.

Snapping his mouth shut, Aleksi withdrew his hands. "I'm sorry."

Kale raised his eyebrows in challenge before grinding against Aleksi's covered cock. "I'm not some fainting flower, Aleksi. I needed to think it through, but I'm yours if you want me."

Aleksi blinked then Kale recognized the familiar feline twinkle of mischief in the man's eyes. "No, mate. You are definitely not a fainting flower."

"Hmm. I like it when you call me mate." He rubbed his nose against Aleksi's, because it felt right, and grinned when the man beneath him purred.

He moaned when Aleksi took hold of his hips again and let him experience the strength and power in those hands. Even the hint of claws didn't stop him from humping against Aleksi's stomach. It actually made it better, adding a little suggestion of danger. He knew Aleksi would never hurt him.

Kale gasped. "Naked. Now."

They scrambled to get up and out of their clothes but as Aleksi started to move toward the bedroom, Kale pushed the big man back down into the overstuffed green cord chair. "Too far away. Here's better."

"Are we ever going to make it to a bed?"

Kale smirked, grabbing the packet of lube out of the pocket of his pants before dropping them back to the floor.

This time Aleksi smirked and nodded at what he held. "Confident?"

"Hopeful," Kale answered, settling astride Aleksi's lap again.

The skin-to-skin contact was dizzying. He attacked the packet of lube and ripped it open. The slippery contents landed with a splat on Aleksi's steely abs. Kale groaned in frustration while Aleksi laughed. Leaning down, Kale lightly bit the shifter in punishment.

Aleksi growled and bit him back, careful to only nip, not injure. "I bite back," the shifter warned.

"Good."

Kale went to scoop up some lube into his hand, but Aleksi beat him to it, swiping two big fingers through the translucent gel then reaching behind Kale to tease his crease. Aleksi ringed his hole then pressed in with one finger, slowly.

"More." He liked the burn and when Aleksi granted his demand, Kale's thighs shook with anticipation. He knew how big Aleksi was. He'd been barely able to fit the man in his mouth. He couldn't wait to feel his shifter spreading him wide, filling him up.

He must have made a needy sound, because Aleksi brought his other hand up to cup the back of Kale's head and pull him down so he could nibble Kale's neck some more. "Shh. Let me get you ready."

Kale grew accustomed to Aleksi's two big fingers. Finally, Aleksi withdrew them. With Aleksi's teeth gripping his neck, he kept him in place as Aleksi reached between them to scoop up more lubricant. Kale's patience was wearing thin. He needed Aleksi *now*.

Aleksi returned to finger Kale's ass. This time he worked three huge fingers inside him. Instinctively, Kale pushed up onto his knees and stuck out his ass, arching his back.

His thoughts scattered when Aleksi let go with his teeth and started kissing Kale's neck. Working over his chin, Aleksi continued over his cheeks and finally claimed his mouth. Kale sank his fingers deep into Aleksi's hair, keeping Aleksi in the kiss until they had to break apart and gasp for breath.

The first pump of Aleksi's fingers urged Kale to let out an unmanly squeak. When Aleksi thrust them deeper, Kale wiggled and drew in a sharp breath as Aleksi rubbed the bundle of nerves inside Kale.

"Oh, God." It left him shaking and his dick painfully erect.

Kale summoned some strength from his need and frustration to pull back and untangle his hands from Aleksi's soft golden hair.

With one hand, he reached down between them and grasped Aleksi's huge shaft firmly. Then, with his other hand, he scraped up the remaining lube and spread it liberally over Aleksi's cock. He wrapped his fingers around Aleksi's dick. Kale's mouth watered. He wasn't a size queen, but he appreciated a large cock for the work of art it was — especially when it was as thick and perfect as this.

Thankfully, he'd grabbed a XL sachet. Kale might like the burn, but that didn't mean he wanted to be ripped in half. Taking advantage of his position, Kale kept stroking Aleksi's cock until the man shuddered and groaned.

"Stop teasing," Aleksi chided, thrusting his fingers deep and tapping Kale's prostate in retaliation.

Kale lifted off Aleksi's fingers and allowed the shifter to grip his hips and position him over Aleksi's dick. He kept absolutely still when he felt the tip press against his opening.

With his gaze firmly melded to Aleksi's, they stayed like that for a few breaths, staring at each other and taking in the moment. This was their mating. After this, he would belong to Aleksi. And Aleksi would belong to him.

After a moment longer, Kale realized Aleksi waiting for him to make the next move, giving him a way out if he'd changed his mind. *Silly shifter.* Kale was surer than ever about becoming Aleksi's mate.

He put his hands on Aleksi's big shoulders and braced himself. Taking a slow, deep breath, he relaxed his muscles. Cramps during sex were so unattractive. He could imagine rolling around on the floor while Aleksi stood there, erection pointing accusingly at him for ruining the fun.

Aleksi must have realized Kale's thoughts were becoming absurd, because he shook his head and chuckled softly, snatching a kiss then whispering in Kale's ear. "Be calm, my mate." And just like that, Kale settled.

He couldn't help clawing his fingers into Aleksi's shoulder as the man pushed the head of his cock inside Kale. Thankfully, the shifter didn't seem to mind. If anything, Kale would say his lover liked it owing to Aleksi's soft growl and full-body shiver.

Slowly, he sank down onto Aleksi's erection, biting his lip until his ass came to rest on Aleksi's pelvis. "Oh. So *full*." Wide-eyed, he looked at Aleksi. Completely focused on Kale, the shifter's eyes had turned pure cat.

Aleksi lifted him up by the waist until Kale thought Aleksi was going to pull out completely, but instead the shifter slowly brought him back down again, sinking inside him once more. It was like a slow torture, building him up to anticipate hard and fast thrusts to match the intensity in his lover's eyes then being forced to accept slow and gentle penetration until he was ready to throw Aleksi down on the floor and have his way with the infuriating shifter.

"Stop fucking around and fuck me!" Kale growled.

That seemed to be the sign Aleksi was waiting for. He slid his hold on Kale's waist down to his hips and tightened before lifting him and then keeping him still, Aleksi's cock only halfway in.

Instinct made Kale hold on and no sooner had he tightened his hands on Aleksi's shoulders did the shifter begin thrusting upward into Kale. The force of Aleksi's thrusts caused him to lose his balance but he caught himself again just in time for the next slamming drive.

Aleksi was still in the chair but seemed to be holding himself up with his legs and shoulders as he kept throwing his big body upward. The display of how strong Aleksi was, even without straining, made Kale shiver. It was a turn-on he'd never experienced. Maybe one day he could get Aleksi to fuck him like this without the chair, just leaning back against a wall or maybe against the wall, holding Kale up with his cock.

"Oh fuck," he shouted.

The fantasies vanished under a wave of sharp pleasure as Aleksi changed his angle and started to bring Kale down as he thrust up again. Kale screamed as the alteration allowed Aleksi to hit the button inside him with every plunge. Kale tried to move with Aleksi but the shifter tightened his grip on Kale's hips, stopping him from contributing. Kale had no choice but to hang on and try to drag in enough oxygen in so he wouldn't pass out.

Aleksi bit down, sinking his sharp teeth deep into Kale's neck. The shock of pain, followed by an overwhelming feeling of rightness and connection with his lover sent Kale crashing over the edge and headlong into the most powerful orgasm of his life. Liquid heat seared his insides as Aleksi came in an explosive climax.

Kale collapsed onto Aleksi, making the chair creak in protest. He was actually surprised the chair had held up under such abuse.

Kissing the bite mark on his neck, Aleksi sleepily said, "*Mine.*"

"Yours," Kale agreed with a tired smile.

Chapter Eight

Sooner rather than later, Kale had to get up and pee. It took some wriggling and maneuvering but he finally got free of Aleksi's arms. Fast asleep, Aleksi had curled around him as much as the chair would allow. Just like a cat—if that cat was six foot ten and covered in bulging muscles. He looked back over his shoulder with a goofy grin. Aleksi was his now. As his bladder reminded him why he'd woken in the first place, he hotfooted it to the bathroom.

He took care of business and washed his hands, smiling when he felt the twinge in his muscles. Being sore in places he hadn't been in years and in some new places too was nice.

Kale caught himself grinning in the mirror and blushed at the dreamy expression on his face. The bite mark on his neck was big but already healed. Aleksi had licked it to form the mating mark. Reaching up to finger it lightly, he shivered at the zing of arousal it caused.

The sound of ringing interrupted his exploration and he ran to the bedroom to answer it before it could wake up his new mate. He grabbed the phone from his pants and, seeing it was Caleb's number on the caller ID, he answered.

He probably had another job offer to consider. His brother certainly knew how to get the best deals from all the squabbling designers on the circuit. Caleb had to beat back offers and bribes from other models to come work for them. No one knew that everything Kale made, he split it evenly with Caleb then they distributed a good chunk of the money to the various charities. So it was almost impossible that they were offering a better deal, even if his brother would ever consider leaving him, which he wouldn't. Kale also received offers from agents, but he gave the same response Caleb did — brothers stick together.

"Hey, bro. You finished with your meeting?" He craned his neck to look into the sitting area and see if Aleksi was still asleep. Sure enough, the shifter was still sprawled awkwardly in the chair. Kale would have to wake him up in a moment or his mate would be suffering for it later. People Aleksi's size were definitely not made to sleep in chairs.

"Hello, my beautiful boy. Are you having fun playing our little game?"

Kale's blood ran cold. "How did you get my brother's phone?"

Immediately racing over to Aleksi, Kale was about to reach out and wake him when Not-Barry's voice cackled through the phone at him.

"Ah-ah-ah! Now *don't* even think about fetching your pussy cat. This is between you and me."

He froze, scanning the room for some kind of camera, but he had no idea what he was looking for. Nothing stood out.

"As for how I got your brother's phone, I've had him in my care since last night. Now listen to me very carefully. You've been a naughty boy, running away from me." Excitement filled Not-Barry's voice as it gradually rose higher and Kale realized the man was enjoying this, even getting off on it.

"You *will* come to your brother's room. Take the elevator directly to the lobby then come here and ride the car straight up without stopping on the other floors. I'll know if you do. You have five minutes."

Panic struck him, but he struggled to keep calm and think. He desperately hoped the man was lying and Caleb was going to walk through the door any minute and ream him for causing so much trouble or for leaving his socks on the floor — any mundane shit.

"I want to speak to my brother," he demanded in what he hoped was a strong voice. Not-Barry's words about not stopping on the other floors confused him. They were on the first floor. If Not-Barry didn't know that, then perhaps he didn't know where they were. However, knowing that Kale was going to tell Aleksi and that Aleksi was asleep told him that Not-Barry was watching him.

Sounds of rustling and a heavy thump came over the line. He could hear Not-Barry telling someone to be good and speak. Kale stopped breathing as he waited, his heart in his throat.

No one else spoke in the background, only Not-Barry. There was another thump and a cry of pain. This time Kale heard the distinct sound of a hand slapping a face and he recognized the voice of his brother cursing.

"Stop it," Caleb cried.

"Tell your brother to be a good boy," Not-Barry demanded harshly.

"No, don't come here, Kale!" Another slap and thump followed, then everything went quiet.

"Caleb!" He quickly shot a glance over to Aleksi to check that the shifter was still sleeping.

"Now, are you going to be a good boy?"

Kale swallowed the bile in his throat. "Yes."

"Yes, what?"

"Yes, sir," he said through gritted teeth.

Not-Barry let out a sickening, gleeful laugh. "Good boy. Now hurry. Time is ticking. Tick, tick, tickity tock."

The dial tone sounded like a foghorn in Kale's ear.

He quickly dressed and, subtly as he could, he typed a message and saved it as an alarm to go off in ten minutes. If he was really being watched then he needed to think of a discrete way of leaving a sign for Aleksi. The shifter wouldn't sleep much longer if he wasn't there. He dropped the phone on the bed under the guise of tripping over his suitcase then quietly walked to the door and left, closing it behind him with a shaking hand.

The elevators were all busy so five of the minutes Not-Barry had given him slipped away far faster than Kale anticipated as he took the stairs. Sneaking past Gio, who was stationed by the front desk, was more challenging. Luckily, Kale was able to dodge behind a giant rubber tree and duck through the door as the officer looked his way. He had no idea if Gio had seen him, so as soon as he exited the hotel, he ran as fast as he could while cutting through the busy crowds.

"Excuse me." He glanced at his watch and started to sweat. Three minutes left. "Out of the way!"

The lobby of his original hotel was more difficult to get through as he entered via the revolving doors. He knew there were officers assigned there by Aleksi's friend, so he grabbed one of the umbrellas from the stand to the left inside the door, opened it up and made a show of putting it down and over his arm, skipping to catch up with a young woman who gave him an appreciative glance. He briefly put his arm over her shoulder. As a model, he knew better than anyone that people saw what they wanted to see. In this case, he was a man with his wife struggling with his umbrella.

As soon as they passed the officers and stood outside the elevators, he removed his arm and apologized, sending her a charming smile. She blushed and looked away shyly. He used her distraction to get into the elevator, pressing and holding the button to close the doors until the metal slid shut with a click. He stabbed the correct floor number and held the door closure button again until he heard a beep. It would ensure the elevator went straight to that specific floor and would not stop anywhere else. Another glance at his watch made the hair on the back of his neck rise. One minute left.

The numbered buttons lit up one by one as the elevator ascended. Kale was practically vibrating by the time Caleb's floor button illuminated. He squeezed out before the metal panels had fully opened and ran down the corridor to Caleb's room, hammering on the wood. "I'm here. I'm here!"

The door swung open before he'd finished shouting.

Kale's feet carried him into the room before his brain caught up with his body.

Slumped unconsciousness, Caleb sat tied to a chair, face swollen and bloody. If Kale hadn't recognized his brother's electric-blue shirt, he wouldn't have even known it was his brother. He started toward Caleb with a cry of anguish, but the sound of the door slamming and locking behind him made him spin around to face Not-Barry.

Shirtless, and with his jeans undone, Not-Barry stood, holding a gun pointed on Kale. Before Kale could react, the man squeezed the trigger.

"Now we can find out how much fun you can take, my pretty, *pretty* boy."

Sharp pain in his arm shocked Kale and he saw a little dart with a pink tuft sticking out of his arm before the world started spinning. He was unconscious before he hit the floor.

* * * *

Stretching and yawning, Aleksi slowly lifted his eyelids enough to scan the room as he tried to figure out what had woken him. He stood and called for his mate. "Kale?"

No answer.

He took in a deep breath, stopping short when he could smell only the lingering scent of his mate. A beeping noise came from the bed and he spotted Kale's phone lying on the bedspread, vibrating as the screen illuminated.

He walked over and picked up the cell. The first thing he noticed was that the device was unusually hot. It was a new model and there was no reason for it to be heating up. The battery was low too, even though he knew Kale had charged it only hours ago. Aleksi snarled as he realized Not-Barry had somehow managed to tap or hack the device. When the note for the alarm appeared on the screen, Aleksi gripped the phone so hard the little glass screen cracked.

NB has C at other hotel. NB wants me or he'll hurt C. Come save us!

From the time stamp on the alarm, he knew his mate had only left minutes before he'd woken. Forcing down his initial instinctive, furious need to hunt down his mate immediately, Aleksi calmed himself and placed the phone on the bed. He continued walking through the room and headed to the bathroom as if nothing was wrong, carefully not looking at the cell's front-facing camera lens.

Aleksi stayed in the bathroom for a few minutes, thinking about the message Kale had left. His mate was smart to leave him clues but he was still going to redden Kale's tight ass when he got his paws on his mate.

Leaving the bathroom, he wandered casually over to the windows and closed the blackout curtains, plunging the room into darkness. The phone's cameras would be useless now. However, Aleksi's cat eyes were as adept in darkness as they were in sunlight.

He threw on his jeans, shoes and shirt and ran out of the room. If Kale was already in Not-Barry's clutches, it wasn't likely the man would be monitoring the camera feed closely enough to see the small flash of light where Aleksi had opened the door to leave.

If he was, all it would do is give Not-Barry a warning. There was no way he was leaving his mate in the hands of a killer for a moment longer. He didn't bother going down the stairs, jumping over the bar instead and landing easily. After bursting through the fire door, he headed for the emergency exit of the other hotel.

Using the handle was overrated and it was almost certainly locked anyway. Aleksi shouldered through the steel-bolted doors as if they were a paper, sending the thing flying several yards down the corridor. It made a horrendous scraping sound and clattering racket but he focused on his next move. Bracing his knees and flexing his hands, Aleksi jumped and grabbed hold of the metal banister on the stairs between the first and second floor and then repeated the move, leaping deftly from floor to floor.

Reaching his target, he threw his body over the bar, bending his legs to absorb the impact, and land silently. Scenting the air revealed nothing, but he hadn't expected it to. He inspected the door that led to the corridor and his instincts told him Not-Barry wouldn't leave it unsecured. He could only imagine what the bastard had told his mate to make him leave without waking Aleksi. He felt the madman would have a backup plan in case Aleksi followed or Kale wasn't able to keep him at the other hotel. Moving to a secondary location with Not-Barry could be fatal because it would take Aleksi more time to track them down.

The modern-style door looked as normal as all the others in the sleek establishment. If anything, it was a little too clean, the shiny metal fingerprint free. This was a good hotel, but even the best didn't clean their emergency exits this well. No one used them or noticed them unless there was an emergency. He stepped closer until he stood about three feet from the door and inspected it more closely. There was nothing obviously wrong and that made him more suspicious. Not-Barry had been very careful with the tear gas bomb and the police set-up. Both incidents exhibited premeditation.

Whatever was wrong here was making his cat even more agitated.

Aleksi tipped his head to the side and tried to single out what specific detail was making him want to shift and bite the metal barrier standing between him and reaching his mate. His animal didn't understand technology. It came from a long, *long* history of beasts that existed and dominated before such things were ever thought of, and although his species had adapted and evolved, there was still that distrust and unfamiliarity with technology and electricity.

"Electricity!"

As soon as he said the word, it made sense — the hum in the air and the spotless door. He crept closer, careful not to touch anything, and the buzzing grew louder. A human wouldn't hear it but his tiger could. It sounded like a stereo system now that he could single it out from the rest of the noises.

Aleksi looked around and spotted a junction box. He walked over to it, then he ripped it open. From the labels, Aleksi concluded that it controlled the lights and electric supply to the floor.

He pulled out the wire for the air conditioning and exposed both ends, stripping away bits of the rubber insulator with his fingernails. Moving back to the door, Aleksi bent and touched both ends to the metal at once.

Immediately, sparks flew and he dropped the wires, kicking them away, growling. Not-Barry had electrified the whole fucking door, guessing Aleksi would take the stairs instead of the elevator. Judging by the violent reaction, there was enough power running through the thing to knock him on his ass. He wouldn't have been getting up again, even in his stronger tiger form. It would have killed him and any unfortunate human who might have come across it.

Aleksi stepped out of his shoes and inspected the soles. There were thick rubber layers on the soles, enough insulation to stop any circuit forming and keep the electric current from jumping to him.

He put his hands in his shoes then wasted no time in slamming the door open. He caught it with his shoe-clad hands before it made any more noise and hoped the racket would pass as someone closing their room door a little too enthusiastically. He lowered it to the ground and noticed a box the size of a book attached to the doorframe.

On first look, it would appear harmless, but Aleksi's keen eyes saw the little lightning symbol on it, the symbol that was right next to the serial number that he recognized as US military. *Where the hell is Not-Barry getting these things?* He discarded his shoes, leaving them by what remained of the door and quickly ran back to the junction box. There, he flicked the switch labeled hall lights, plunging the corridor into darkness with just the exit sign glowing green. On his way back through the doorway, he let his claws free and slammed them into the little box, reducing the electrifying device to mere pieces of plastic and screws.

He caught the one piece he wanted with the serial number on it and slipped it into his pocket.

Aleksi jogged down the corridor, watching and listening hard in case there were more traps. He didn't expect any, however. Not-Barry was too arrogant not to think his backup plan would work, but Aleksi wasn't taking any chances. Luckily, Caleb's room was almost at the other end of the floor to the emergency stairs so there was little chance Not-Barry had heard him.

He froze as he reached the correct door and he heard a laugh that sent shivers down his spine. Aleksi had seen many things, done many things—both right and wrong—but that laugh frightened even him. It scared him because he knew his mate was inside with person who had made it.

A whistle and a crack from the other side of the door made his blood run cold. He knew that noise. It was the sound from his past when he'd been captured as a young boy and forced to perform as a freak in a freak show until he had grown strong enough to escape.

It was a whip.

He listened again and flinched, a tear running down his cheek when he heard Kale crying out— screaming—even though it was muffled. *Kale must be gagged to stop him from making too much noise.*

All the training as a thief, soldier, mercenary and eventually a bodyguard hadn't prepared Aleksi for the grief or fury that swamped him at the sound of his mate in pain. He was so overwhelmed with violent emotions that his tiger almost broke free. No one responsible would survive his fury, his teeth or his claws.

Shaking himself, Aleksi squared his shoulders and strained his hearing, listening for the arc in the swing of the whip so he could determine where the wielder stood in the room. Aleksi guessed Kale was on the bed from the sound of the cries, presuming Caleb's room was the same layout as Kale's had been. There was another desperate voice shouting a few feet from the door. It must be Caleb.

Everything in him demanded that he break down the door and simply storm in but Not-Barry could have a gun or some other weapon aimed at Kale. He heard footsteps and the whistle of the whip kept changing direction, as if the person was moving around the room.

Whistle. Crack. Scream. The pattern repeated once more. Hopefully, if Not-Barry was holding a second weapon, the man would spin round and point it toward him instead of Kale.

Moving faster than he ever had in his life, Aleksi crashed through the door. He made as much noise as he could, ensuring he had Not-Barry's full attention. Bullets ripped through his side and he jolted with the impact.

Not-Barry stood between him and his mate, so Aleksi reached for his feline abilities and leaped over the gun-wielding man. Aleksi lost his breath as he slammed into the floor. Quickly getting back to his feet, he planted them firmly and kept himself between Kale and danger. Now Not-Barry was nearest the door, with Caleb in a chair to the right and Aleksi's mate safely behind him.

Not-Barry fired again and again, reaching for another gun that had been tucked the jeans waistband and emptied that one too. Aleksi was fast—fast enough to get to Not-Barry and kill him before any of the bullets hit him. However, with Kale tied to the bed, it would leave his mate defenseless. Even just one stray bullet could take his mate's life.

With no choice but to be a shield for Kale, Aleksi stood and accepted the pain as bullet after bullet pierced into his flesh, tearing him apart. Not-Barry backed toward the door. From his peripheral vision, Aleksi saw Caleb had managed to get free from his bindings, but Aleksi didn't look away from Not-Barry.

Caleb must have taken advantage of Aleksi's arrival to tip over the chair and himself.

Not-Barry ran out of bullets but the crazy man kept clicking the trigger as he backed away. Caleb grabbed a heavy decorative lamp from the side table with both hands and managed to raise it as Not-Barry backed up.

A hard strike knocked Not-Barry out and the stalker crumpled to the floor. Caleb stood next to him, beaten and bloody, but strong and panting with exertion. "No one messes with my brother."

"*Polizia!*"

The corridor lights turned back on and Aleksi tried to blink away the spots in his vision. Police officers flooded the room. He hissed at the ones crowded around him and Kale. They offered help while simultaneously telling him to get on the floor.

He ignored them all and turned to stagger over to the bed. Breaking Kale's handcuffs with a flick of his wrist, Aleksi collapsed to the floor beside the bed. Blood poured from his wounds and left a trail behind him. His mate's face was contorted in agony and pressed sideways into the mattress. Blood covered Kale's back. There was almost nowhere to touch him that didn't look damaged. In the end, he settled for gently wrapping his hand over Kale's ankle and purring softly. Kale jumped and tried to get away from his touch. His mate immediately calmed, clawing closer to him instead. "I'm here, mate."

Aleksi shouted Gio's name, knowing his friend would be amongst the cavalry. The police must have heard the gunfire.

"Only the human on the floor is a threat. Secure him," Gio snapped angrily before looking at him and seeing all the blood. "Call an ambulance. Now!"

The last of Aleksi's energy left him, bleeding out like the red trail running from the many gunshot wounds in his body. Aleksi reached for Kale. Everything was fading and he couldn't stay upright.

He needed to protect his mate. Danger. His mate was in danger.

"He's shifting!" Gio shouted.

The panic in his friend's voice was the last thing he heard.

Chapter Nine

Kale blinked awake then screwed his eyes shut when the bright lights hurt them.

"Kale?"

Caleb's voice sounded far away but he felt pressure on his hand as if someone was holding it. Something cold touched his lips and he darted his tongue out to catch it as his throat started to burn from dryness. The little bit of moisture from the ice chips was like ambrosia and he opened his mouth for another spoonful.

"The nurse said you can only have a bit at a time." Despite Caleb's words, his brother gave him some more.

Kale moaned as the cold soothed his throat and cracked lips. He opened his eyes again and frowned. Everything seemed wrong but he couldn't quite figure out why.

"No, Kale. You need to stay like that until the doctor checks you out. He usually stops by around this time," Caleb said.

It was then he realized he was lying on his stomach and the reason Caleb's hand felt odd was because of the angle. He tried to remember what had happened, but things were rather fuzzy and in bits and pieces mixed with black periods he couldn't remember.

He did remember Not-Barry had called, saying he had Caleb and Kale had gone to a hotel room. Everything after that time was blurry and disjointed with flashes of himself screaming as fire raced over his back and ass.

"You okay?" His voice sounded rough and broken.

"Me?" Caleb asked. "I'm fine."

Kale gave him a stern look—or what passed as one when he was lying on his stomach, glaring up at his brother.

"Really. It's just a few bruised ribs, a broken nose and a split lip," Caleb admitted, shrugging and unsuccessfully covering a wince after the motion.

"Heard noise. From your room in the morning." He couldn't say anything more. Ever since he'd received the phone call from Not-Barry, he'd been terrified that something had happened to Caleb that time wouldn't be able to heal, something that Caleb might not be able to come back from.

Caleb obviously got his meaning, because his brother went even paler and looked at the door as if he were contemplating running away.

"He...uhh...he ordered a prostitute and dressed him up in your clothes, then he made the man shower in stuff he stole from your room to smell like you. He fucked the man and strangled him. The police found the body in your room where he'd arranged his victim on the bed so the man looked like he...like he was sleeping instead of..." Caleb coughed, wiping away the tears.

His brother hadn't cried since they'd lost Garrick. "Caleb—"

"No. No talking about what happened until we're home and I can drink my way through our scotch collection."

"Sounds like a plan," Kale agreed with a sigh. Scotch sounded really good right about now. Aleksi would be impressed by their collection. The shifter had mentioned he liked a glass of quality alcohol once in a blue moon.

Panic struck him in the chest when he remembered gunshots and Aleksi getting hurt. The memory was fuzzy, there was a lot of blood on the floor, soaking the beige hotel carpet.

"Aleksi. Where's Aleksi?"

"Your bodyguard is in the shifter wing. He's alive, healing well, but still mostly out of it because of the amount of damage. He almost shifted and he was going feral. The police almost had to shoot him with tranquilizers, but somehow you managed to talk him down, even half-conscious. I swear to God, I've never seen anything like it. He stood in front of you and the gun and he didn't move a muscle as all those bullets ripped into him. Then he wouldn't let any of the police near you until the paramedics got there and some guy called Gio promised to look after you. For the past two days, there's been three guards posted outside your room."

Kale almost puked at the images Caleb's description called up. He hadn't seen what had happened but he could imagine and piece together the sounds he remembered. "Days?"

"Yes. It's been two days since…"

Ignoring the pain in his back and Caleb's fussing at him frantically to lie back down, Kale pushed up on his hands and gingerly shifted his legs until he was sitting on the bed, his legs dangling over the side. He shook with the exertion and he had to grit his teeth to keep from crying as his eyes filled with tears of pain.

"Dammit, Kale. Why don't you ever do what I tell you to do?"

"Because I'm your little brother and it is my solemn duty to be the biggest pain in the ass possible," he joked, forcing a laugh as he looked up at Caleb's worried face.

He wasn't the only one with wet eyes as Caleb grabbed him into a hug, pulling back when Kale yelped, but he held on and refused to let Caleb out of the hold. "I was so scared when he said he had you."

"I told you not to come," Caleb chastised.

"Of course I was going to come, you asshole." Kale smacked Caleb on the arm. He cursed when the action tugged at the whip marks on his back. Pushing away, he must have accidently poked Caleb's damaged ribs as his brother hissed in pain too. "Sorry."

They stayed in silence for a moment as Kale breathed through the throbbing until it faded to a bearable level, thanks to the morphine drip in his arm. Thank God he hadn't pulled that out when he'd decided to move.

As soon as he caught his breath, he held his hand out to Caleb for support and tried to ease his feet to the floor.

"I need to get to Aleksi."

Caleb frowned but took his hand and fretted over him as they got him to his feet. As his weight settled, Caleb asked, "Why is he so special to you? Is there something more between you than sex? You don't usually do relationships."

Kale looked at Caleb in surprise. "You knew we were sleeping together?"

Caleb shot him an exasperated smile. "Please. I'm surprised you had enough restraint that you didn't jump on him in the office when he first walked in. You've always had a weakness for muscles. Though, I get the feeling there's more to Aleksi than muscles."

Rolling his eyes, Kale gasped as his weight settled and the wounds on his back stretched "He is. I'm his mate," he confessed quietly, flinching when his brother spun around, almost knocking him over.

"Shit, sorry. Are you serious?"

The incredulous tone didn't exactly sound encouraging. "Yes. We'd just...claimed each other before..." He wasn't sure how to explain something he didn't really understand himself. He and Aleksi were essentially married in the shifter way and Kale felt the overwhelming, aching need deep in his chest to be with Aleksi.

Aleksi would have been with him if he were able. His tiger mate was more than a little possessive and wouldn't trust his safety to strangers. They hadn't exactly had a good and trust-inspiring experience with police lately. "We're mated and now I need you to help me get to my mate."

For a second, Kale was worried Caleb had had some sort of mental breakdown. His brother just stared at him open-mouthed then Caleb hugged him gently. "Congratulations, little brother. I'd give the obligatory speech about not knowing him and this is all too fast but I saw how much he cares or he wouldn't have taken those bullets for you. You were all he was worried about." Caleb ruffled his hair as he used to do when they were younger. He then unhooked the wheeled stand for Kale's drip from the wall and carefully wrapped an arm around his waist for support. "Let's get you to your man."

* * * *

Getting his police guard to let him go down and see his mate had been harder than he'd thought and had taken almost an hour. He was still being chased by nurses, tutting and muttering words that Kale thought were unprofessional. Italian was a beautiful language but he only knew the bad words, thanks to a birthday book from his brother on how to curse in ten languages. Kale hadn't expected nurses to be so foulmouthed.

At least he was finally in the shifter ward now. There were armed guards on every corner that their police escorts had told them carried several different types of tranquilizers, ready to knock out most shifters in the event that they became lost to their animal natures.

To be honest, Kale hadn't understood much of what the doctors and guards had explained to them and he was more than a little freaked out. He wanted to go back home to Aleksi's house and forget everything that had happened but at the same time...he didn't.

The fact that Aleksi had been hurt protecting him was something he was going to have to come to terms with, along with how dangerous Aleksi's job was and the issues of be committing to a relationship with a predatory shifter.

Before Aleksi, he'd never had to think about these things. Did it make him a bad person because he'd hesitated at Aleksi's room?

"Come on. He's on the other side of the door. You heard his doctor say he's doing fine and that he woke up around the same time you did. It must be something to do with your mating bond thing. The doctor said there is no reason he should shift." Caleb probably thought he was nervous in case Aleksi lost control, but that didn't even enter into the equation.

The tiger didn't scare him anymore since he'd cuddled with the beast at Aleksi's house. Kale remembered talking Aleksi down from unintentionally shifting before coming to hospital and passing out.

Kale just needed to know he was enough, that he was going to be a good mate and not a burden. The police escort and the guard unlocked Aleksi's door and held it open enough for Kale and Caleb to slip inside before closing and locking it again, securing it with a strong metal grate. The same grate covered several other areas, including the air vent and the window to the corridor where the guards were looking in.

"He's not going to shift," he assured his brother, when Caleb hovered by his side nervously.

His voice must have woken Aleksi because his mate's eyes snapped open. The second Aleksi looked at him and groaned, Kale was all but running toward his mate—or at least hobbling clumsily with Caleb's help. Aleksi's doctor had said they could stay with his mate only as long as they didn't make Aleksi worse or let him move.

However, Aleksi, with his damn shifter nose, must have known Kale was in pain and Kale knew it was only a matter of seconds before the stubborn man was up and coming over to him. So Kale forced himself to rush the last few feet to his mate before it could happen.

"Hey. I'm here. It's okay." Wiping the sweat beading on Aleksi's brow, Kale perched on the side of his mate's hospital bed so he wouldn't fall as his body shuddered and shook. His doctor had only allowed him to visit after Kale had lied, saying he was feeling much better already.

He brushed his hand through Aleksi's hair and looked down with blurry eyes at the mass of bandages covering his bare chest and stomach. The shifter made a mewling sound like a cat denied its food or something it desperately wanted. Kale entwined their fingers.

"Up."

Touching Aleksi helped dissolve some of the doubts and fears because he was just so damn happy that his mate was alive and well enough to be bossing him around. Aleksi somehow heaved his big body over a few inches, giving Kale enough room to get onto the bed next to him.

"No. You're hurt," Kale forced out, wishing he hadn't let the doctor call his bluff and remove his pain-relief drip.

Aleksi bared his teeth and pouted, making Kale laugh despite the pain at the ridiculous of it.

His mate smiled tiredly. "Need you. Up."

He looked to Caleb for some sort of help but his brother just shrugged. "I'd do what he says, bro. Cats get pissy when you don't listen to them." With that, Caleb snagged a cushion that had fallen to the floor and balled it up under his head as he settled down to sleep in the chair in the corner of the large room.

Kale shot his gaze up to his mate's, worried how Aleksi would take his brother's teasing, but Aleksi was smiling, his eyes soft with amusement and affection. If Caleb relaxed enough to tease you, then he liked you. Caleb had never teased anyone Kale had dated. If he wasn't on the verge of passing out again, he would have pumped his fist in the air.

"Fine," he huffed, slowly wriggling farther onto the bed and easing back against the soft pillows. He winced as the lashes on his back protested but it felt good too, as he had been lying awkwardly on his stomach for two days.

Aleksi wrapped an arm around him and Kale let himself sink into the heat Aleksi was giving off.

"I was so scared. I thought I was never going to see you again." Saying it aloud brought it all to the fore again. Even though he still couldn't remember everything that had happened, he remembered being scared. Scared he couldn't help Caleb, scared he wouldn't see Aleksi again and scared that the dream of having a home and something real and meaningful dangled in front of him like a carrot was going to burn to ashes around him.

At first, he thought Aleksi wasn't going to respond, but then his mate purred deeply and lulled him into a peaceful sleep. Just before sleep claimed him, he heard Aleksi say something in Russian and kiss his head.

Chapter Ten

Aleksi slowly came awake to the sound of quiet snoring.

He rolled his head on the pillow to see Kale fast asleep with his head hanging back on his arm that was around the man. Kale's mouth was open and Aleksi felt a small damp patch on his arm where his mate must have drooled a little.

"You're making goo-goo eyes at my brother. Eww. Please tell me you don't think the snoring and drooling thing is *cute*."

Aleksi turned to see Kale's brother sitting in a small armchair, looking tired and uncomfortable. He stretched his neck and winced when it cracked.

"It *is* cute," Aleksi defended, smiling when Kale snored louder for a second before settling into a quiet slumber again.

"Yeah, right. You're sunk, bro."

"Bro?"

"Kale said you've mated and according to the Internet on my phone that means you're basically married and it can't be broken. You can't cheat, because your animal won't let you and you'll always protect him, even with your life. I saw the last one for myself."

Aleksi watched as Kale's brother cleared his throat and glanced away, plucking at some imaginary fluff on the arm of the chair.

"I would do anything for him and my tiger loves him already." Usually he wouldn't be so candidly honest with his feelings with someone who was a stranger. But Caleb was offering him something precious, a place in the small, loyal family consisting of the two brothers.

Caleb finally looked at him again. "Thank you." The man's face changed from serious to curious and Aleksi realized the two brothers were more alike than probably either of them would like to admit. "You're a tiger? Can I see?"

The innocent question and the excitement he heard and smelled from the man made him smile. "My tiger is a little different from the ones you've seen on The Discovery Channel or in a zoo. I'm a saber-tooth tiger and if I changed in here, there wouldn't be any room for you and Kale to breathe. Once I'm healed, I may be persuaded to shift so you can meet my cat."

As Caleb's eyes grew wider and wider, Aleksi wondered if he should have broken the news of what he was more carefully. "Holy freaking duck balls bouncing on a bicycle. That's so cool!"

Laughing, Aleksi had to put a hand on his stomach so he didn't bust any of his stitches as he wiped tears from his eye. He'd never laughed so hard before but it was simply the sheer amazement and excitement on the man's face. It was definitely not the reaction he usually received.

He supposed it wasn't every day someone met a saber-tooth tiger shifter in the regular human world view of things. Wolves were a dime a dozen and there were other shifter races that were courting the media to experience the limelight. But most of the rare races still hugged the shadows because they had big, fat targets painted on their asses. Shifter hunting and trade was as common as human trafficking, but there was hell of a lot more money involved — tens of millions more.

He sobered and checked on Kale. Aleksi suspected Kale had actually woken several minutes ago and was pretending to sleep in order to listen in on Aleksi and Caleb interacting with each other. His sneaky mate was eavesdropping.

Any other time Aleksi would probably call him out on it and tease him but he imagined Kale was concerned about how they would get on, so he didn't rat him out. "Kale, wake up, mate."

Kale made a show of yawning and nuzzled into Aleksi's chest, careful of the bandages. The last thing he wanted to do was hurt Aleksi even more.

He opened his eyes and peeked up at Aleksi, only to see the shifter staring down at him with a knowing look. "Shit," he whispered, hiding his face as he blushed at being caught eavesdropping. It had just been too tempting to listen in. Whatever. No one had ever accused him of being a stickler for etiquette.

"Hey, you're awake. You know, you drooled all over your pussy cat, right?"

His brother laughed at his own joke, but Kale was mortified. He wiped his mouth. Maybe if he prayed hard enough, the ground would open and he could hide in a hole until everyone forgot that he had drooled on his lover.

"No name calling or I might decide to eat you when I shift."

Caleb's smile died and he went pale before scowling. "No eating your brother-in-law."

Kale gave up on the whole escape route and sat up as the need to move and take the weight off his back took over. Even though he didn't want to leave the warm, comfy embrace against Aleksi's side, where he was snuggled up tightly, the injuries on his back were starting to sting and ache too much for him to stay there.

"Help me up, please?"

Caleb shot up and over to him, taking his hand and pushing Aleksi's away when Kale's mate tried to help. "You can't help until your doctor clears you. He said you'll heal quicker than we do, but until then, you aren't to so much as sneeze, or we'll get kicked out of here and Kale will throw a tantrum."

Kale growled, offended by the dig. "I do not *throw tantrums*."

"Oh, no? Then how did we get in this room with your mate?"

There was no chance in hell that he was giving Caleb the satisfaction of being right. Kale was prepared to play devil's advocate and argue the sky was green if he had to. In his own defense, Kale had had to do something drastic or else he would have been ignored and never allowed to visit Aleksi.

The moment the doctor had caught sight of his tears and the mating bite mark on his neck, everything had changed. The doctors and guards had been all too eager to help Kale get to Aleksi. But he was sticking to his guns. He had *not* thrown a tantrum. He'd merely pointed out that it was to their benefit to let him be with his mate. Otherwise, either Kale would find Aleksi himself or the more dangerous option could happen — Aleksi could come looking for him.

Pushing his advantage, Kale had also mentioned that Aleksi's tiger was very possessive of him and wouldn't like it if anyone smelled like Kale. That was before he'd deliberately brushed up against the doctor who didn't want to let him go to his mate. When persuasion tactics didn't pay off, blackmail usually did the trick.

"Have you been causing trouble, mate?" The shining gold-green of Aleksi's eyes revealed the tiger liked that he'd fought to get to his side.

Unfortunately, Caleb chose to be chatty again and told Aleksi the whole story, smirking when Aleksi growled at the part where Kale spread his scent on other people. "I better not meet that guard," Aleksi threatened dangerously. "However, you're right. I would have ripped the hospital apart to get to you if you hadn't have come to me when you had. I was just waiting for the doctor to finish his rounds so there would be fewer guards for me to incapacitate."

Hearing that Aleksi would have come after him lifted a weight he hadn't noticed had been sitting on his chest. "Well, I saved you the trouble, then."

Kale pulled harder on Caleb's hand until his brother got the hint and offered him his arm to use as a hook to hang onto. "Thanks. How are your ribs? They're not Tic-Tacs, you know."

As he stretched his legs and got the blood flowing again, it eased some of the buildup of pressure, relaxing his angry muscles.

Wincing, Caleb laughed, reached into his pocket then took out an orange pill bottle and rattled it at him. "Don't hate me. You could have had your own little bottle of magic pills, but you pissed your doctor off."

"And you could share," he shot back with a glare as his injuries started aching. He kept pacing slowly in the hopes that the pain would ease off again.

"I would, but you know you're allergic to aspirin."

He sighed and nodded. He should have been more diplomatic when he was trying to get to Aleksi. Impatience had always been one of his flaws. Going back to his doctor to apologize wasn't an option since that bridge was well and truly burned. "I know," he sighed. "I don't like you drugged up. You think you're *down with the kids*."

To Kale's embarrassment, his older, sensible, straight-laced, always serious, manager brother stuck out his tongue and did the rock-on hand signal. "Whazzzup!"

"Oh...my God." Kale shook his head and started laughing even though it hurt. He glanced at Aleksi and the humor froze in his chest. Aleksi was definitely not laughing. "Are you okay? Are you hurting?"

Aleksi sat upright in the hospital bed. Wincing, Kale could only imagine how much it must have hurt to do that with all the bullet wounds scattered over the muscular torso and stomach. One bandage blushed red in several spots.

Kale rushed back over to the bedside. "You're bleeding. Caleb, get the doctor!"

"I am fine, mate. Did your doctor really refuse to give you pain medications? Pain from lashings is a mix of a burn and a cut and hurt. You doctor should never have let you go anywhere without pain management."

The look on the shifter's face sent a chill down his spine.

Paling, Aleksi started shaking and there was a thin sheen of sweat glazing his brow. Aleksi pushed a lock of blond hair behind his ear, looking agitated. Kale put his hand over Aleksi's and turned it over to trace the lines on his mate's palm. Aleksi immediately calmed and Kale kept doing it until Aleksi leaned back against the pillows again.

His back was on fire as he moved and the fabric of his shirt scratched at him more like it was wire wool instead of light cotton.

"I'm fine. You're fine." Before Kale could really say anything else or do anything to comfort the shifter, there was a noise at the door. Aleksi growled as the guard cleared away the door grates and stepped inside, followed by a man wearing a vest that looked like the Kevlar ones S.W.A.T teams wore on crime shows underneath his white coat.

"Hello, I'm Dr. Sanders, how are we feeling?" The doctor, in his forties maybe, stood shorter than he was, but wider built and more muscular than the doctors Kale had seen in the other part of the hospital.

"I'm fine." Aleksi waved off the man. "Check my mate. He's in pain," Aleksi instructed firmly.

Dr. Sanders raised his eyebrows.

"You are not fine, Mr. Cooper, but I can see why you are concerned about your mate." The doctor took the stethoscope from around his neck and approached Kale, running his gaze over him in a way that made Kale feel like every nook and cranny was being assessed and filed away.

"Cooper? That's not Russian," Caleb pointed out, ever the tactful pothead.

"Scott's brother, Robert, found me, gave me a home and trained me. I took Robert's middle name as my last when I joined their family because that's the name Robert uses on missions. A few of the others did the same actually, when Robert rescued us."

Aleksi flicked Kale's brother a glance but had turned to look at Kale when he answered. To be honest, Kale had wondered the same thing too, but he didn't want to ask the man he'd basically married what his last name was. It was ridiculous.

There was no more explanation from Aleksi, but Kale hadn't really expected that much from his stoic mate, especially with other people in the room.

"Mr. Andrews, is it?"

"Yes, Dr. Sanders," he answered obediently as he was poked and prodded. He turned around without a word of protest when he was directed to remove the borrowed hospital scrubs. He glanced at Aleksi but the man's face was set stubbornly, waiting for Kale to do as the doctor directed.

With help, he managed to get the shirt off and he eased the elastic waistband of the paper-thin pants down so the back was just under his ass and the front still covered his private area. The last thing he wanted to do was flash everyone.

"The wound is clean and although the area is swollen, I don't foresee long-term issues past the healing period. How do these feel on your lower back and buttocks?"

Running his inspecting fingers gently over Kale's ass and back, Dr. Sanders made a non-committal *hmm* noise. Kale couldn't stop himself from flinching away from the doctor's fingers.

"Sorry."

"No need to be. Frankly, I am surprised you were allowed to leave your bed at all. Where is your pain medication?"

Kale winced again "I don't have any. There was a morphine drip in my arm when I woke up a few hours ago but a nurse took it out before I came down here. I needed to see Aleksi." He added the last part defensively when he glanced over his shoulder to see the Dr. Sanders scowling, his expression dark.

"Are you telling me that your doctor did not give you anything for the pain?"

"I told him I felt better than I did," Kale admitted reluctantly, not looking at Aleksi when the shifter hissed quietly. "Stop it, Aleksi. You're scaring the guards."

In truth, the guards hadn't moved much, just readjusted their grips on their tranquilizer guns, but it probably wasn't best to test their restraint.

"Are you allergic to any medications?"

"Yes, aspirin, but I don't take other pain killers if I can avoid it because it irritates my stomach."

"Okay. I'll go e-file a prescription. I recommend an anti-inflammatory to reduce the swelling from your moving about and an anesthetic spray to numb the area for you. This is a serious injury, Mr. Andrews. I appreciate the need to see your mate. I have worked with shifters for a long time now, but you could have seriously set back your recovery by pushing your body too hard." The doctor stepped away from him, picked up the medical clipboard from the bottom of Aleksi's bed and started scribbling notes.

Feeling chastised, Kale redressed then sat on the edge of the bed. For someone who had slept for two days, he was exhausted. By the time he refocused on the conversation, the doctor had unwrapped Aleksi's numerous bandages and was examining them.

"It seems that you are healing exceptionally well. I suggest we leave the new dressings on for another few hours until my next visit then we can discuss when you'll be fit for travel and the like. I would say that your animal nature is particularly resilient. There are very few races that can heal this quickly. If I didn't know you had been with us for two days, I would say that these wounds occurred weeks ago." The doctor gave Caleb a quick onceover as well, suggesting that his brother stay in the hotel opposite the hospital tonight instead of sleeping crammed up in the uncomfortable hospital chair.

True to his word, the doctor left then returned a few minutes later with an orange bottle for him and a spray for Kale's back. It must have been clear that Aleksi wasn't going to shift or lose control. The guards left quietly and didn't re-engage the door grates. The doctor's visit had obviously confirmed that Aleksi wasn't a shifting threat.

"Hey, you have a view." Caleb's statement made him realize the room actually did have windows. They had just been covered with similar grate to the door, but these had to be controlled remotely because they were retracting to reveal a nice view of the city.

If they weren't in a hospital, this would probably be a tourist trap.

"How far down do the injuries go, mate?"

Kale tensed at the question. He'd managed to keep his face to Aleksi throughout the examination so Aleksi still hadn't seen his wounds.

"You need to apply the numbing spray." Aleksi's voice left no room for Kale to wiggle out of it or change the subject. Caleb had seen the injuries when he'd been unconscious but *he* hadn't seen them, so he didn't know what they looked like. He only knew they felt massive, as if the whip Not-Barry had stuck him with had flayed him wide open and the doctors hadn't sewn him up yet.

"Caleb can do it," he said, holding the spray out to his brother. He gave Caleb a pleading look.

Caleb frowned and stared at him for a long moment. His brother must have figured out that he was stalling so that Aleksi didn't see his back. His brother jumped up from the chair and headed to the door. "Sorry. I need to go to the bathroom. Aleksi can do it." No one would have guessed Caleb had busted ribs by the way the traitor all but sprinted out of the room.

"Kale. Why don't you want to show me?"

"Because I don't know what they look like and I don't want you not to want me anymore, okay? I almost lost you and I don't want you to be disappointed that I don't look like the person you mated." Until Kale started spewing out the words, he wasn't sure what he was going to say, then he just couldn't stop. "I'm so sorry. It's all my fault. Caleb was abducted, beaten and subjected to watching that sick fuck dress a hooker up like me, wearing my underwear and using my shampoo and body wash then he strangled he poor guy. You were shot — *shot!* — because of me, and all those people Not-Barry killed are on my conscience, stains on my soul. You deserve better." Kale sobbed, finally breaking down and covering his face with his hands as he sat heavily on the plastic chair next to the hospital bed.

"Kale. Come here."

Shaking his head, Kale continued to scrub away the tears streaking down his face. It *was* all his fault. If he hadn't made a target of himself or if he'd simply let

Not-Barry get him the first time, then the real Barry would still be alive and so would the police officers, the prostitute and Caleb, and Aleksi would be fine too.

"Kale, stop thinking like that right now! We would definitely *not* be fine. Yes, those people might well have been alive but they could just as easily have been hit by a bus or have died a million different ways at any second. Caleb would have lost his baby brother, his only family. And I would still be alone and searching for a mate I was never going to find, because my other half is you. I *deserve* you."

Kale looked up through his fingers and saw Aleksi had gotten out of bed and was kneeling in front of him.

"You have to get back into bed before you pop a stitch or something." Kale tried to lift Aleksi by putting his hands under Aleksi's arms and pulling, but the big shifter didn't move at all. "Aleksi, please."

"I want you to say that what Not-Barry did was not your fault. I want you to say it to me and you then I want you to show me your injuries so I can apply the spray the doctor gave you." Aleksi looked into his eyes as he spoke and the intensity of the stare unnerved Kale.

Since he'd woken and come down here with Aleksi, he had started to feel an echo of Aleksi's emotions. It wasn't anything intrusive or controlling. In a way, it was comforting to know he wasn't alone but it also meant that Aleksi would be able to feel his emotions too.

"You can't always get what you want," he said hotly, wiping his face in his arm so he could see clearly.

Aleksi just laughed, making Kale even angrier.

"I am a cat, love. Eventually, if I want it bad enough, I get exactly what I want." Aleksi leaned in and kissed Kale gently.

The corner of his mouth tugged upward but he pursed his lips to kill the smile threatening to come out. "I'm serious, Aleksi. Get back in bed. Right now."

"You know what to do to make me do what you want."

Glaring, Kale stood up and tried again to lift Aleksi, grunting when it was like trying to move a two-ton rock. On second thought, the rock would probably be easier to budge.

"Fine!" He stood then paced for a moment and tried to hold on to his anger. The shadow in his mind flared again, as if it were nudging him, and he realized it was Aleksi trying to show him something.

It was as if he'd stepped into a warm hug when he accepted the nudge. The happy feeling covered him like a blanket. "This was not your fault," Aleksi coaxed, standing then invading Kale's personal space again. Aleksi framed Kale's face with his big hands, keeping him from trying to escape Aleksi's searching gaze.

"It wasn't my fault," Kale said it quietly and tried to pull away.

Aleksi held fast and started stroking his temples. "Again."

"It wasn't my fault," he repeated in a stronger voice.

Aleksi's eyes sparkled and Kale was mesmerized. "I love you," Aleksi asserted.

The words rolled off Kale's tongue before he understood what he was saying. "I love you — *what!*"

Aleksi danced away too agilely for someone who had been shot almost a dozen times, laughing happily, as Kale swatted at him half-heartedly. It was bad form to hit someone who had taken multiple bullets for you.

Aleksi grinned victoriously. "I knew you liked me."

A punch in the face was really too good for some people. "Are you twelve?"

"No, just a little lightheaded from moving about too much," Aleksi said honestly, looking a bit wobbly.

"Get in the damn bed," Kale ordered, annoyed at how calm his mate sounded about being hurt. He ushered the shifter back to the bed and wondered if he could get the doctor to loan him some restraints so he knew Aleksi would sit still.

"I've never tried bondage before."

Aleksi's comment made him stumble and the only thing stopping him from face planting on the floor was Aleksi grabbing his forearm, steadying him.

"Don't *do* that," Kale said.

"Do what? You were the one talking about restraints."

If Kale had thought dealing with Caleb when his brother was hopped up on pain pills was embarrassing, this was mortifying. Being shot and drugged was turning Aleksi into a naughty, sexy, temping...pain in the ass.

To hide his embarrassment, Kale retrieved the anesthetic spray and thrust it out toward Aleksi. He turned around and whipped the scrubs shirt over his head before he could chicken out. The pain caused by the quick movement helped him to get over his awkwardness. This was the first time he'd ever said 'I love you' to someone he wasn't related to and he was trying really hard not to freak out.

In his head, falling in love had been part of the plan. Agreeing to mate Aleksi had been a big risk. Kale might have been teased into saying the words, but in his heart, he felt them. Damn tiger had gotten his way again.

Aleksi knew he should probably feel guilty about playing dirty to get Kale to say he loved him. Honestly, he hadn't expected Kale to repeat his declaration or that he'd have to scent the truth in Kale's words.

He would let Kale have his space for now but not for long. With a dozen new bullet holes in him, Aleksi thought he was entitled to be a little bossy. He hadn't lied when he'd said he was lightheaded. Rapid healing was something to be thankful for at times like this, but it had its own consequences, such as a drunk feeling, and his lips tended to be looser than he'd like — such as could his declaration of love. Aleksi had had a long-term plan to woo the human and make Kale fall so in love with him that he would never want anyone else.

That was out of the window now. He came out of his thoughts when he noticed Kale had come back to the bed shirtless, holding something out for him. "Will you do my back for me, please?"

Aleksi snatched up the spray before Kale changed his mind.

Kale swallowed loudly. Aleksi scented the nervousness giving way to fear as his mate hesitated and half-turned so he couldn't see his mate's back.

"I love you," Aleksi said again, this time without the playfulness.

Kale nodded and twisted around slowly. Aleksi could see the tremors racking the man's body.

The pain of being shot was nothing compared to the agony that stabbed through him at the sight of all those angry red and purple lines marking up his mate's beautiful skin. He held his breath when Kale lowered his waistband and Aleksi saw the marks going down from the curve of Kale's shoulders to the tops of his thighs.

He knew first-hand how much injuries like that hurt and he mourned for the little bit of light that he knew had dimmed in his mate for going through that trauma.

"How is it?"

"Fine. I don't know what all the fuss was about," he said with a flat tone. One of his brothers would have simply smacked him and grumbled about him being an ass.

Grimacing at the realization that Kale might not understand his dry humor, he tried to think of a way to backpedal.

Instead, Kale surprised him again and laughed. It wasn't a snort or a polite laugh but a full belly laugh. Aleksi drew in a deep breath, confirming that his mate was genuinely amused by his scent. He breathed a sigh of relief at that, thoroughly aware that his thoughtless words could have backfired.

"They aren't too deep but the way the lines cross over one another are what is probably causing you the most pain as the skin heals and is pulled in several directions."

"Does it look as ugly as I think it does?"

Aleksi knew Kale's sense of worth was significantly tied to his appearance, so he didn't give a speech or cliché line about beauty was on the inside. Kale's career depended on how he looked. His mate did have a good reason for being concerned, but he had a feeling it was more to do with how Kale thought Aleksi saw him than anything else.

"I suppose if you squint and tilt your head, it looks like one of those strange paintings that sell for millions of dollars."

Kale snorted. "Will the scars bother you?"

"Do mine bother you?" Aleksi knew he only had a few that were still visible. Shifters didn't scar easily, especially ones as big as he was. The bullet wounds would take a while to fade since there were so many of them.

Kale tried to turn around, but Aleksi clamped a hand on his mate's waist, moving so he was sitting with his feet on the floor but his weight on the bed.

"Of course not!" Kale replied.

"Then you have your answer. Scars are what remind us that we were strong enough to live through pain."

"You think I'm strong?" Kale sounded as if it was a foreign concept to him.

Aleksi was really going to have to drill it into his mate that he was amazing and worth a hell of a lot more than his looks. "I think you're very strong, mate. I'll be sure to write you a list of all of your attributes when we get back to our home."

"Our home?"

"You said it was one of your conditions for mating with me," Aleksi teased. The idea of sharing his sanctuary with another person still bothered him, but Kale wasn't just a person. Kale was his mate. Aleksi was looking forward to waking up with him every morning and going to sleep with him every night.

With a little push and concentration, he sent the feeling of contentedness through the link that was starting to form between them. The closer they grew, the tighter the bond would be. It was why he'd remained unconscious until Kale had awoken. Aleksi and his tiger had felt that Kale needed them and had fought their way through the mental barrier of the sedative Aleksi had been given. His doctors had certainly had a fright when he'd woken up roaring Kale's name.

The blush working its way up Kale's neck was too tempting for him and he leaned forward gently to kiss his mate's skin, mindful of all the wounds. "Mine."

"Yours." Kale relaxed.

Aleksi started purring in an effort to keep the man calm as he treated the wounds.

Drawing back, he read the instructions for the medicated spray. According to the leaflet, he only had to point, squeeze and reapply in four to six hours' time. It applied easily and Aleksi saw a difference within a few minutes as Kale relaxed his muscles and loosened as the spray began to numb the area.

Leaning forward as much as he could without stressing his own injuries too much, Aleksi blew a cool line of air over the damp skin of Kale's ass. The scent of excitement filled his nose and Aleksi grinned, tracing his fingers along Kale's hipbone before teasing the neat patch of hair above Kale's cock. If Kale were to turn around, Aleksi would be in the perfect position to swallow his mate down whole.

Kale swallowed loud enough for Aleksi to hear it. "Aleksi, what are you doing?"

"Showing my mate how much I want him," he replied, getting hard at the thought of giving Kale pleasure.

Snapping upright, Aleksi snatched his hand away from his mate, in case he had to unleash his claws. He didn't want to cut Kale. His tiger stiffened inside him, warning him predators were nearby and his gaze shot toward the door. He let a smaller version of his saber teeth descend. As he was injured, he wasn't taking any chances that the threat could harm his mate.

Aleksi groaned when he saw who was outside his room.

He watched as Kale glance up to see what he was looking at and paled. Aleksi could just imagine what Kale thought, as the group of scary looking men peered through the door window.

The party of onlookers was completed with Caleb. Everyone except Caleb was staring right at his mate's bare ass and his tiger gave a growl of warning to his brothers.

"Sorry." Kale blushed, visibly trying to regain his composure as he dragged the scrubs back on. The rushed action made Kale hiss and flinch as the back of the shirt hit his injuries. The spray hadn't had enough time to dull the skin completely. He'd gotten carried away when the pain had started to recede.

"Be careful, mate." Taking hold of the shirt, Aleksi gently rearranged it so it didn't touch Kale's injuries.

"I just didn't want you to think..." The way Kale ducked his head and tugged at the clothes gave Aleksi the idea that maybe Kale misunderstood why he was growling.

"You're a model, Kale. I know that I am going to have to get used to people seeing your body. I'm possessive and protective, so I do not relish the thought of scratching my brothers' eyes out for ogling you, but I'll never growl *at you*, okay?"

Obviously reassured, Kale nodded. Aleksi even got a small smile before it vanished and Kale's eyes turned dark and sad. "I may not be a model anymore. My doctor said there will be extensive scarring on my back and ass."

"Not necessarily," Khan, one of his brothers, said loudly from outside.

"How did they...?"

Tapping his ear, Caleb then slipped inside the room but Aleksi's brothers remained outside. From his possessive display, his brothers would definitely know Kale was his.

"Shifter hearing," Aleksi and Kale said together, smiling.

Aleksi waved his brothers in.

"I see your assignment is going well," Scott said drolly.

Aleksi rolled his eyes and ignored the knowing looks from his bothers as they spotted the claiming bite mark on Kale's neck. His mate turned to share a concerned glance with Caleb. No doubt, his mate was wondering if Aleksi planned to tell his boss and family about them.

"That reminds me. We really need to have a talk about how this bodyguard thing works. You see, I actually have to have a body to guard." Aleksi pinned Kale with a hard look before smiling to diffuse the tension.

Kale rolled his eyes. "I'm sorry. I'll work on that."

The snarky reply made him grin. Having his ass handed to him later for getting shot was going to be fun. Kale was stunning when his eyes were bright with anger. As soon as Kale had had time to digest everything that happened with Not-Barry, his mate would be back to his fiery self.

"Good," he accepted with a secret smile.

Huffing, Kale walked back over to him.

Aleksi waited until Kale sat on the bed next to him. He put his arm around his man before turning back to his friends. "Everyone, this is my mate Kale. Kale, these are my friends, my brothers. Raptor is the bald one, Dean is sporting the mohawk, Harris has the short brown hair and Merlin is the one with long black hair, while Iago has the orange-and-red curls. Finally, Viktor is the ice blond." He went round the room, pointing and naming his friends and shaking his head, as they seemed to take his introductions as an excuse to pull faces or flirt outrageously with Kale. Aleksi would give them a few minutes to laugh it up and have fun but after that, he would see how fast his brothers really were and if any of them could outrun an angry saber-tooth tiger.

"What did you mean, Khan?"

"I mean that my venom can be altered and has proven to be very successful in the reduction of scarring. The medical trials have been very promising."

"Medical trials?"

Nodding, Khan explained, "Yes, there was a doctor trying to track down rare venoms. I contacted him and said I'd be willing to help. I've been working with him a few months."

Aleksi didn't like the sound of that. Even though shifters were a recognized part of society now — with rights and protection laws — that didn't mean they were safe. Rare shifters still had big black market price tags on them. "Are you sure that's a good idea? Are you being safe?"

"I'm not sleeping with him, Mom," Khan replied with a smirk.

Somehow, Aleksi knew Khan was holding something back. Aleksi and the rest of his brothers looked at Khan. They seemed just as surprised and worried at the news of Khan getting involved with a doctor who was conducting medical trials.

"Khan," Aleksi started, unamused with Khan's attempt at a joke.

Khan tensed but sighed when it was clear none of them were going to budge on the subject until they knew he was safe. "I'm taking precautions. It's all anonymous and I'm keeping an eye on his work by acting as a courier. He doesn't know who I am. Rob checked the doc out and I did my own research too. I even broke into his lab and his house when he wasn't there to so I could poke around. He seems legit."

Aleksi nodded and took Khan at his word.

"Okay then, just keep being careful." He hugged Kale closer when he felt his mate getting lost in the conversation. He knew he'd have to explain the risks and dangers about the fact that they had enemies. Aleksi was hoping to convince Kale to train to defend himself. It wasn't realistic to think he would always be by Kale's side to protect him—as bitter as that was to acknowledge.

Khan nodded to him and turned to Kale, speaking to his mate. "I will. Now...your mate's wounds are actually at the perfect stage to start the treatment for the best effects. The only problem is that the treatment will take about two months to be completed and there's another month of aftercare too. However, from what I've seen of the doctor's work, your mate shouldn't have anything but faint shadows at the end of it."

Kale jolted beside him and Aleksi worried that his mate was going to pin all his hopes on this option.

"Are there any side effects from the venom?" Aleksi wanted to be one hundred percent sure that the experimental treatment wasn't going to harm Kale in any way.

Kahn shot him a look but continued talking to Kale. "There haven't been any severe negative side effects. One person said the application of the venom solution gel stung and another experienced hair loss. However, both subjects also scored highly on the psychological test that measured how likely a patient was to exaggerate symptoms. There were also reports of mood swings and aggression from those who took the medicine orally."

On the surface that was better than Aleksi had feared, but his tiger still wasn't thrilled with the idea. Kale must have picked up on his lack of enthusiasm. His mate leaned away from him. "Do you not want me to do it?"

Even though he considered an angry Kale incredibly hot, not even he was stupid enough to fall into that trap. No, he didn't want Kale to do it, but he understood why it was important to Kale and his career.

"It's your decision." He knew as he said it that Kale wasn't going to let this drop but he couldn't think of anything better to say.

Kale hit him with a hard stare. "That's not what I asked."

Aleksi's brothers backed away, sniggering from their direction.

"This is something you need to decide," Aleksi hedged.

"This affects you too," Kale pointed out, biting on his swollen bottom lip.

Aleksi realized now that it wasn't a shy characteristic but something his mate did to hold back that viscous tongue of his.

All this talking about his feelings was beginning to tear down his front of being a stoic, emotionally repressed Russian. He'd worked hard to maintain that stereotype. Chatty protectees were worse than the stupid, obnoxious ones.

Aleksi grabbed Kale, gently bringing him closer as he captured his mate's mouth with his own. This was a much better way to deal with things. Kissing Kale could make him forget the world.

One kiss extended into two and soon Aleksi wasn't thinking about the hospital, their wounds or the issue of Khan's experimental treatment. It was only a retching noise that brought him back to the room and he realized he was massaging Kale's growing cock behind the thin cotton of the scrubs.

"Uh. Can you *not* molest my brother when I'm in the room?" Caleb made a gagging sound at the end of his complaint.

"You can always leave," Aleksi offered, chasing Kale's sweet-tasting lips.

Kale laughed and pushed him back, pulling the hospital blankets up to cover their waists. It might have disguised their erections tenting their hospital clothes but nothing could hide the thick scent of desire in the air. Aleksi decided not to bring up that fact and let his mate think no one had noticed. It was the least he could do since he was the reason for the uncomfortable situation.

"I would if I had anywhere to go. I forgot to get the number of the hotel next door while I was milling around the front desk waiting for you two to talk it out," Caleb said.

"We booked rooms. You can stay with us if you want to." Viktor extended the offer freely

Aleksi smiled. He wanted his family to like his mate and new brother-in-law.

Caleb visibly relaxed. Aleksi got the feeling his brother-in-law would feel much better with them after the trauma of the abduction from a hotel room. He caught Viktor's eye and motioned discretely to Caleb. Viktor looked at Caleb, then nodded and moved closer to him.

Kale squeezed his hand and mouthed 'thank you' as Caleb walked out of the door with Viktor and Raptor. Aleksi squeezed back. Dean, Harris and Iago blew him kisses as they exited. Scott remained behind.

"Rob gave me a message to pass on," Scott said quietly, handing him a small piece of paper.

A

I taught you better than to get shot. Heal up and take some time to be with your mate. Don't worry about the stalker.

R

Aleksi tilted the paper so that Kale could read it and shrugged when Kale gave him a questioning look. Robert only dealt with threats to his family one way. Aleksi hoped Not-Barry got what he deserved because somehow the man was clearly connected to powerful people and he had a bad feeling that Not-Barry wouldn't see any jail time once extradited to the States.

He turned back to Scott with a scowl. "How does he always know?"

"I'm not sure. The most popular theories are some sort of microphone tracker, a ghost spying on us or that he's brainwashing us into actually telling him everything then we forget that we gave him information." Scott's voice sounded level and serious.

Aleksi snorted a laugh. "A ghost spy?"

Scott held up his hands up and walked backward to the door, making to follow the rest of his brothers and Caleb. "I didn't say they were good theories. Now get better quickly so I can send the rabble back to work. We'll be back later in the official visiting hours."

"Scott!"

His friend and boss hesitated to leave and Aleksi tilted his head slightly. It was such a subtle gesture that only a shifter or someone who'd spent most of their life around shifters would have noticed and understood. It was a submissive pose, but it meant more than that between them. Aleksi was letting Scott know how much he appreciated having him and his brothers come there for him. None of them liked hospitals and more than one of them had been out on assignment so they must have left the job or switched out with another protector to be here.

"Where else would we be when you got your ass shot full of holes?"

Aleksi growled and Kale handed him the hard plastic cup from the bedside table. The empty cup hit the door as it shut quickly behind Scott. His boss shot him the bird through the window and winked.

"Sorry about those clowns," Aleksi said with a laugh. His brothers could be a little over the top if a person wasn't expecting it or used to their weird sense of humor.

"What do you mean? They were great. I'm impressed they all managed to get through security outside of visiting hours." Kale's sincere smile made Aleksi relax.

"Come on. Let's get some sleep before they invade again." Aleksi shuffled back and rearranged the mound of pillows behind him before settling and finding a comfy spot. He patted the space on the bed.

As if on cue, Kale yawned so wide Aleksi heard the man's jaw click. "Okay, but just for a little while," Kale stressed. "You owe me more kisses."

"I do?" Aleksi didn't know why he was arguing but he was curious.

"Yes, for getting hurt," he answered with a smirk.

He wrapped one arm around Kale and smiled sleepily as his mate curled into his side. "Oh. Well, I suppose that's fair."

Chapter Eleven

A few days after his brothers had turned up, Aleksi was ready to pull out his hair by the time his doctor finally signed him off as fit to travel. Caleb informed the charity shoot organizers of what had happened to Kale. Apparently, they had been so eager to get his mate on board with the shoot that they had reorganized and delayed the whole thing in order to have Kale participate.

So now, Aleksi was back in a familiar situation, standing in the shadows, watching Kale half-naked and covered in makeup with other models, both male and female, draped over his body.

Aleksi had been surprised to learn that it wasn't just one charity this photo shoot was for, but several, as part of a new campaign to reach a wider array of people. It included a TV advertisement for domestic abuse awareness and discrimination, as well as magazine shots to improve body confidence in teenagers. Some of the advertisements had been shot using a handheld digital camera with the models wearing no makeup and holding black rectangular pieces of card like sensor bars over their genitals.

He had to admit that he'd been skeptical at first. However, seeing the way the models and charity staff were regularly stopped during the shoot to make sure Kale was okay or whether he needed a break, had changed his mind. Perhaps the fashion world wasn't as cold as he'd thought. Egos seemed to have been left at the door for this campaign.

Kale's bruises had actually helped with the domestic abuse image the director was going for and Aleksi had to admit that the photos he'd seen on the monitor looked amazing. Even with real bruises and makeup bruises, Kale looked stunning and drew Aleksi into the photograph. He didn't even register the other almost-nude models in the photo or the ones walking around the set.

The photographer called time and he watched with a smile as Kale untangled himself from the other models and started toward him. Aleksi tensed when one of the male models tried to get Kale's attention and Aleksi shifted his claws, gouging his palms as he fought to stay where he was and not pounce on the nude model. His anger quickly gave way to amusement as Kale just walked right on by without giving the model a second look.

Since leaving the hospital, they'd been staying with Caleb in a safe house owned by Robert in New York. The brothers didn't want to be separated yet and none of them were enthusiastic about the prospect of staying in hotels any time soon.

Kale's nightmares were starting to ease off. They'd started in the hospital and Aleksi had taken to staying awake to stand guard and protect his mate from the fears in his mind.

"I think we're done here. I can't believe they waited for me, I'm so glad to be a part of something like this." Kale stopped walking when their bodies almost touched.

Aleksi felt the heat and excitement coming off his mate. What he wouldn't give for a soundproof room right now.

"You're thinking naughty thoughts," Kale accused, stroking his fingers over Aleksi's chest.

That was something else he was beginning to notice. Kale would tease him and seemed to light up when Aleksi would always respond or when they would talk about different things, anything from the TV programs they loved to what their plans for the future were.

The beginning of their relationship had been mostly based on sex and Aleksi would be lying if he said he hadn't been worried about whether their personalities and interests were compatible. He shouldn't have worried. His mate was perfect, even if Kale did have a strange fascination with films like *Sharknado*. Now there was eighty-six minutes of his life he was never going to get back, but watching Kale becoming so animated over the film was interesting.

After suffering through the first film, Aleksi was hoping that the rumors were false and that the producers weren't planning a trilogy. If they were, Aleksi might have to go and ask one of his brothers to shoot him to avoid watching it.

"The photos looked good." He wrapped his arms around Kale's waist and let himself look at his mate. Part of him still couldn't believe he was mated or that he was happy about it. However, his tiger was more content than ever. The possessiveness took some getting used to but at least he was beginning to manage it better.

Kale's eyes lit up as he asked, "You really liked them?"

"Yes. You are stunning. I didn't think there was that much thought or effort that went into producing glossy photos for advertisements and billboards. You must have done three hours straight on the three different campaigns and each photo was just slightly different, a quirk of a lip or more intensity in your eyes." He hoped Kale understood his explanation.

Kale grinned at him and the next thing Aleksi knew he had his arms full of Kale who was hugging him tightly and pushing his face into Aleksi's neck. "You *get* it."

It was only then that Aleksi realized that this had been a sort of test — albeit a subconscious one — since Kale wasn't the type to play mind games. As Kale pulled back, there was a different kind of lightness to his mate now that hadn't been there before.

"I think so," Aleksi began. "This is what you love to do — to be a part of creating something with what and who you are and sharing your ideas with a photographer to make it amazing instead of good. That's what you really want to do, isn't it?" He wasn't sure if his answer was right or not or even if he properly understood what he was saying. But it was the truth.

"Yes." Kale turned a lovely shade of pink.

"Okay. You said you were going to take a break from modeling while you were on Khan's treatment, so let's look into how you'll do that. I'm sure Caleb will help." There was no way Caleb wouldn't want to go in the new direction with Kale. The man was loyal — and strong. The man had knocked Not-Barry out before the psycho could do any more damage and the Italian police had carted him off. Aleksi wouldn't forget that debt.

Scott was keeping him apprised of what was happening with the case, but Aleksi was worried about what Robert had written in the message for him at the hospital. He didn't want Robert getting involved, at least until Aleksi knew for sure whether the rumors were true that Not-Barry would plea bargain. He was waiting on confirmation from his contacts.

His mate frowned and Aleksi feared he'd presumed too much.

"I think you're right, Aleksi. Caleb has been bored for a while now, so this is probably the right time out to experience something new. I bet he'd love trying his hand at photography."

* * * *

As they tumbled through the door, groping and rubbing against each other, Aleksi threw his house keys in the direction of the kitchen. He'd find them later.

He swooped in for another kiss as Kale broke away to suck in a desperate breath.

Aleksi slid his hands up Kale's shirt, careful not to touch his mate's back. The healing scars were still tender to the touch and he didn't want to ruin the moment. Everything had been so hectic since coming out of hospital. First with the Italian police interviews, the photo shoot, then the FBI interviews — they hadn't really had a moment to themselves. By the time they got to bed most days, they were too tired to do much more than cuddle.

Leading Kale to the stairs, Aleksi noticed his mate casting anxious glances at the door behind them. Aleksi made a mental note to get Oscar, the company security tech, to install an alarm system. Of course, he'd blindfold the bear shifter first. Aleksi was okay with his brothers knowing where his sanctuary was, but that was it. Besides, Oscar would understand. The shifter was the same with his caves.

"Have I told you how much I love your home?"

Moaning as Kale bit his lip, Aleksi tried to think.

"Our home," he responded.

He dragged Kale, giggling and gasping, to the bedroom,

Since being mated, his tiger had become more balanced and playful, not as concerned with asserting dominance. His brothers were coming over in a few days to welcome them home. Kale was cooking. But Aleksi had a backup plan. Something told him Kale's skills in the kitchen were less than stellar.

Bouncing on the edge of the bed, Kale abruptly stopped laughing as Aleksi began to stalk him.

As he watched, his mate scrambled off the bed and took a step to the side, as if to run.

Aleksi tensed, ready to follow, but Kale simply took another step, then another, until he was in the middle of the room and Aleksi was now the one with his back facing the bed.

Kale began peeling off his clothes and Aleksi paused. Kale had an amazing body and Aleksi wanted to rub himself all over it. The scars and faint, yellow bruises only added to his mate's appeal. The strength and courage it must have taken for Kale to walk into Not-Barry's clutches to save Caleb was incredibly sexy.

The blue silk shirt floated to the floor and Kale started on the low-waist trousers. One undone button revealed the top of Kale's bush and the undoing of the second button confirmed that Kale was going commando.

"Mate," he moaned in agony as his cock hardened even more.

If Aleksi had known Kale was wearing nothing underneath the thin trousers, he would have jumped him earlier and given the FBI more than they'd bargained for. The damn feds were a menace, going over and over statements as if they were looking for a hole in their stories.

Aleksi couldn't look away as Kale slowly bared more of the neatly trimmed trail of hair leading to his crotch. He was hardly breathing by the time Kale stopped teasing him and dropped the trousers to the floor.

When he was nude, Kale gave him a knowing look. Aleksi could be irritated by Kale's amusement, but he had better things to do — such as devouring his mate.

Tugging Kale to him, Aleksi purred and nuzzled his cheek over Kale's head, marking him with his scent.

Kale moaned and rubbed against him. "It's been so long since we've touched."

Pretending to misunderstand, Aleksi pulled back and smiled. "We touch all the time."

Kale called his bluff by cupping Aleksi's erection through his jeans and massaging him firmly. "Want to rethink that?"

"I want you," Aleksi answered, grinding their groins together and trapping Kale's hand between them.

The added roughness of his jeans made Kale shudder and whimper. Aleksi loved to hear the noises Kale made when they played together.

Attacking Aleksi's jeans, Kale gave a good impression of a shifter and growled when the zipper jammed and wouldn't open because of his erection.

Aleksi's patience disintegrated and he ripped the damn things off his legs and clawed his shirt down the middle so he could toss the fabric aside. With nothing between them now, Aleksi was about to sweep Kale up into his arms when his mate beat him to the punch.

Leaping at him, Kale appeared to have no fear that Aleksi wouldn't catch him.

He caught the man easily. "Be careful."

Wrapping his legs tightly around Aleksi's waist, Kale rolled his eyes. "I'm fine. Stop coddling me and fuck me instead."

His mate wiggled and Aleksi was about to ask what was wrong when he got his answer. Letting out a shaky breath, he searched for control. Kale had managed to position Aleksi's cock between his ass cheeks. And every time his mate clenched and squirmed, the tip would brush Kale's asshole.

Without lube to ease the way, the rubbing created delicious friction.

Aleksi's hips hitched without his consent.

"Lube, Aleksi!"

Kale's shout broke through his lusty haze and he sat back so that they were both on the bed, Kale sitting astride his chest. He scooted them up the mattress toward the solid oak headboard.

They reached out at the same time, rolling in separate directions and each rummaging in their bedside cabinets. Aleksi found lube first and lifted it like a trophy.

Snatching the bottle from him, Kale then squeezed out half its contents onto Aleksi's aching cock. "Cold," he commented with a glare.

SA Welsh

His mate straddled his chest again and Aleksi forgot about the freezing gel.

Kale poured more lube onto his fingers and reached behind himself.

Watching Kale stretch himself was highly erotic. He could see the pleasure start to build in Kale's eyes.

Aleksi took hold of Kale's cock and fisted it. He kept his grip loose until Kale thrust into the tunnel of his clenched hand then tightened it until his mate's movements became frantic and he made little whimpering sounds. Trailing his left hand lower, he brushed the back of his knuckles over Kale's testicles. They were heavy and hairless, perfectly smooth like the rest of Kale' skin. The only body hair Kale didn't wax was the neat patch above his cock and the light path to his navel.

It took only a few minutes for Kale's balls to twitch in his hand, but Aleksi was having too much fun to let it end this quickly. Once they had built up their stamina, he'd see how many orgasms he could wrestle out of his mate. Now, however, he didn't possess the control to draw it out long enough to drive Kale to the edge and not push them both over.

"I'm ready," Kale announced breathlessly.

After releasing Kale's leaking erection, Aleksi pulled Kale's hand away and replaced it with his cock. He gave his rigid dick a quick pump to make sure the lube Kale dumped on him was evenly spread.

He gritted his teeth as Kale slowly lowered onto him and his cock was engulfed by tight, wet heat.

Being ten inches long and thick enough that some men couldn't get their hand around his cock meant he had to go slowly with his lovers to avoid tearing them. In the past, he had simply regarded it as a chore, something that delayed the pleasure of fucking.

With Kale, though, this was his favorite part, the agony of staying still and the tension as he shook with the need to pound into the man. The exact moment Kale gasped and clung onto him, fingers curling into Aleksi's pecs was beyond anything else Aleksi had ever experienced. Neither of them looked away or tried to hide from the intensity of their feelings.

"You're so damn big," Kale groaned.

Kale inched down over Aleksi's cock, wearing an expression of eagerness.

As his dick sank inside Kale, Aleksi fought against his instincts to claim and dominate. His tiger roared inside him.

Aleksi's eyes locked onto Kale's tempting mouth. Kale's lush, pink lips were made for kissing, for licking—they were made for him. Aleksi grabbed Kale and slanted his mouth over his, kissing him deep and fiercely.

His gums tingled and he couldn't stop his incisors from lengthening.

Jolting back from the kiss, Kale licked the drop of blood from his bottom lip.

"You bit me," his mate accused.

Eyes, sharpening on the crimson dot. "Sorry."

Kale clenched down on him. "Don't be."

His eyes rolled back in his head at the strangling pressure around his cock. Aleksi whipped his hips upward, driving the rest of the way inside Kale.

They both cried out and panted as their bodies were overcome with the sensation of being completely joined. Kale moved first, planting his hands on Aleksi's chest and rising then slamming back down.

Aleksi thrust up as Kale rode him like a man possessed.

But it wasn't enough.

Placing his hands on Kale's hips, he steadied him, then quick as a flash, he rolled them over so he was on top and Kale lay flat against the mattress.

"Fuck!"

He froze, wide eyed, as he remembered Kale's injuries.

"It's okay. I'm fine. You just caught me by surprise," Kale rushed to reassure him.

Aleksi tried to move back but Kale kept him in place by tightening his legs around his waist. Cradled between Kale's thighs, he had more leverage. He pushed up on his arms and began power-driving into Kale, setting a fast, hard rhythm that made Kale scream for God.

If he had any neighbors, they'd no doubt thought he was killing Kale.

Adjusting his aim, Aleksi gave Kale everything and thrust until his back became damp with perspiration. Kale dragged his fingers down Aleksi's torso.

Aleksi rolled his hips and made certain he hit the spot inside Kale that made his mate go, "Eeeeeee!"

Kale spread his legs wider and arched his back. "Aleksi!"

The tight grip of Kale's body and the way his mate called his name stole his breath. He reached down between them and curled his hand around Kale's cock. Aleksi plunged deeper into Kale's body and shuddered as Kale leaned up to bite his chest.

The move shocked him as Kale's human teeth pierced his skin. He hoped Kale would leave marks. His tiger relished the idea of wearing Kale's bite. Everyone who saw it would know just how much he pleased his mate.

Wide-eyed, Kale flung his head back. Ropes of cum splattered over his chest and the scents of their mutual pleasure filled Aleksi's nose.

His claws burst free of his fingers and his teeth grew, overlapping his bottom lip. His tiger's aggression needed an outlet so he slashed at the pillows above Kale's head. Artificial stuffing flew everywhere. Feather pillows weren't an option. The last thing a predatory shifter wanted to smell when he was making love with his mate was food. That wouldn't end well for anyone.

Aleksi roared as the world exploded around him.

Waves of intense pleasure crashed into him and he pumped his release into his mate.

Collapsing to the side so his weight didn't injure Kale, he gulped for air. Never in his life had an orgasm left him so utterly shaken.

Aleksi kissed the mating mark on Kale's shoulder and settled him closer to his side and out of the wet spot where they'd rolled on the bottle of lube. He'd go and fetch a washcloth from the bathroom in a minute.

"Nap, then more sex," Kale grumbled, already asleep before Aleksi could reply.

Looking over at his mate, he smiled when he spotted the bits of stuffing in Kale's hair.

* * * *

As Kale looked out of the living room window of Aleksi's house in the woods, he heard the bleep of the security system. Every time something bigger than a rabbit crossed the underground sensor barrier Aleksi had installed on the edge of the tree line, a little beep sounded. When the sensor triggered, automatic locks engaged.

At first, he'd thought it was silly, something else to add to the list of things Aleksi insisted would help protect him, but it actually did make him feel secure. It was sweet that the big, bad shifter was so focused on keeping him safe. That more than anything had helped him get over his fear of Not-Barry escaping again to come after him, Caleb or Aleksi.

The sensor wasn't the only change that had been made since Kale had moved in last week. Well, technically he had only brought the last lot of his stuff in that morning and had unpacked it an hour ago. He'd agreed with Aleksi about not having cable or complicated electronics that would run off the generator, but he had managed to persuade the shifter to cave on the Internet issue. The den now functioned as his office and had WiFi. There was also a little plug-in thing he had to use if he needed to go online anywhere else in the house, but Kale didn't plan on using it. He knew how much Aleksi hated the *buzz*.

In return, Kale had agreed to have a tracking chip implanted under the skin of his armpit. He still couldn't believe that he'd let the man chip him like a fucking pet. Aleksi had played dirty, asking him while naked and wet from the shower. At that point, he could have asked Kale to chop off a limb and Kale would have said yes. He had taken revenge, though, and had gotten Aleksi hooked on two vampire TV series — *Blood Ties* and *Moonlight* — despite his mate's denial of it. They often curled up on Aleksi's mountain of cushions when they had an evening free to watch the DVD boxed sets on his laptop together.

Kale waved as he saw Scott and Caleb walking up the path carrying a large crate. By the time he got to the door and disengaged the locks, Caleb and Scott were almost at the front step.

Running out to meet the two men, Kale eagerly greeted them. "Hey, guys!" He grabbed at the label pasted on the crate and ripped it off so he could look at it. "Is this it?"

"Yep, it came this morning and Scott helped me lug it up here. Where's the big guy?"

"Around," he said with a secret smile.

Aleksi was somewhere close. He'd gone to lock up the truck and make sure they'd grabbed everything. Surprisingly, Kale had gotten used to there being no vehicle access here. It made everything that much more relaxing when they actually had time to come out here and away from the city.

Aleksi would have heard Scott and Caleb arrive. If he hadn't made himself known by now, it meant his tiger mate was planning something. Kale was beginning to notice that Aleksi and his tiger were quite playful and liked springing surprises on him.

The tiger had settled so much, feeling secure in being mated, that Aleksi had even managed to go for a run with his brothers in shifted form without fear of hurting them or trying to be dominant. It had been crazy to watch a saber-tooth tiger, a phoenix and an enormous king cobra playing tag in the woods. The minute his back was fully healed, he was going for a ride on Aleksi up into the mountains. They were both looking forward to it.

Over his brother's shoulder, he spotted one of the big oaks swaying at the tree line. Aleksi was too good for the move not to be deliberate, so Kale dropped the label then patted his pockets, swearing. "Damn, I must have lost my phone when I was over by the trees. Can you do me a favor, Caleb, and go see if you can find it please? I want to unpack this before Aleksi gets back."

His brother gave him a weird look as if to say Kale should get it his damn self, but Kale shrugged and did the pouty face that Caleb always teased him about, since it was usually the pose unimaginative directors wanted to lead with. It was guaranteed to get a laugh. Sure enough, Caleb snorted, turned, then jogged toward the trees, laughing. Since they'd come back from New York, Caleb had been bugging Aleksi for days to let him see Aleksi's saber-tooth tiger. Kale just hoped Caleb knew what he was asking for. Either way, they were about to find out.

Scott shot him an inquisitive look and narrowed his eyes at the tree line. Kale knew the man had spotted something when he smiled widely and took out his cell phone, pointing the camera toward Caleb, who was probably going to kill him.

They didn't have to wait long for the show. As soon as Caleb stood a few feet from the trees, Kale heard Aleksi roar and his mate burst from the woods, soaring over the top of Caleb's head with ease. Caleb screamed and stumbled before running back toward the house. Suddenly his brother realized Aleksi stood between him and the promised safety.

"Kale!"

Kale had to take pity on his brother and quickly walked over to where Caleb was now crab-walking backward away from Aleksi, who sat watching them intently and making chuffing noises. Seeing a saber-tooth tiger laughing was the oddest thing he'd ever witnessed but it was also sort of endearing.

"Caleb, this is Aleksi's tiger."

Kale approached his mate slowly and reached out to hold one of his mate's giant teeth. The tooth was so thick he couldn't wrap his hand around it. Kale was glad he was never going to be on the bad end of those teeth. Aleksi dipped his big head for him to get a good angle to give him scritches.

"I hate you—both of you," Caleb swore, shakily getting to his feet and storming back to the house. "If you think I'm carrying anything else up here for you, you're delusional. That's the last favor I do you for a while."

Kale knew Caleb was just blowing off steam and later his brother would be back to bothering Aleksi to see the tiger again. That massive head shrank and a few seconds later, Aleksi stood in from of him, naked and aroused from the adrenaline rush of shifting quickly.

Kale shrugged out of his jacket, wadded it up and threw it at Aleksi. "Cover yourself up."

"Kale—"

Kale raised his eyebrows at Aleksi and unbuttoned the first button of his shirt. "You either cover up or I'll get naked too."

Aleksi grabbed the shirt and held it over his growing erection with a sigh. "I hate it when we have guests."

Sulky wasn't exactly the mood Kale was going for here. If he had his way, Aleksi would be on edge until Scott and Caleb left then Aleksi would be so wound up by that time the shifter would just rip Kale's clothes off and take him up against the wall, maybe even outside.

"I know, but think about how great it will be when they leave and we can test out what's in the crate." He traced his fingertips over Aleksi's chest then dipped them low on Aleksi's belly before turning to walk back to the house.

That immediately piqued Aleksi's interest, as Kale knew it would. Aleksi walked faster and Kale almost had to run to match his strides. When they came to the crate, Kale waved a hand at it. "Be my guest."

He laughed as Aleksi practically attacked the crate, sending bits of wood and splinters flying everywhere, which was going to be a bitch to clean up later. "It's the chair — the one from the hotel in Milan."

Kale nodded. "The chair we mated in. I called the manager and they agreed to ship it here if we promised to never go back there." Really, the woman he spoke to had been less than pleasant but Kale couldn't blame her after they had almost destroyed the hotel and terrified many of the guests with all the police tramping in and out—not to mention the obsessed killer roaming the halls.

Aleksi's face softened and his piercing eyes pinned Kale again.

Since they'd finally gotten the all-clear from the hospital but on strict orders not to overdo it, Kale had discovered that the flashes of tiger in his lover were more than simply little losses of control. When he gazed into Aleksi's eyes and the tiger looked back at him, Kale was just as in love with the animal as with the man, though obviously he expressed his feelings differently.

Even though Kale had gone out of his way to make sure the shifter knew that Kale didn't regret agreeing to the bond, he also knew Aleksi was still wary. He'd wanted to do something that showed Aleksi that no matter what had happened, they were in it together.

The shifter stalked up to him, face unreadable.

"You really got the chair?" The growled tone sounded aggressive.

Out of the corner of his eye, Kale caught his brother stepping forward—maybe to intervene—but Kale quickly put his hand out and made a gesture to tell Caleb that he was okay.

"You said I could get furniture." He laughed, trying to diffuse the sudden tension. Kale backed up as the shifter stalked him.

His breath caught as Aleksi kept coming at him and he kept stepping back. They continued the dance until Kale's back met the wall of the house and he gulped, feeling trapped. It was interesting that he didn't feel the need to get away, however.

Aleksi crowded him, leaning down until their faces were only an inch apart. "You bought *our* chair," he whispered in a breath that blew across Kale's cheek.

"I did," Kale said with a smile.

"Why?"

He stopped the flirty reply ready to roll of his tongue and really thought about the question. "It was the beginning of us—like this. I wanted to remember the time when I decided to give you everything."

Aleksi stepped the last few millimeters closer, their bodies flush against each other. "Everything?"

The Russian accent and the one-word questions growled in his heavy tone sent shivers down Kale's spine. He couldn't look away from the eyes of his lover, both cat and man. The significance of the simple question hit home. He still hadn't told Aleksi much about his life when he was younger or about Garrick, dodging the questions and changing the subject whenever Aleksi asked.

It felt wrong to keep it from Aleksi when he knew any questions he asked the shifter would be answered honestly, even if it were painful. Some of the answers he wasn't ready to hear. But soon he would be strong enough to handle them.

Something had to give. It was time for Kale to invest all of himself and stop giving it lip service. They were mated and he couldn't go back—and he didn't want to

He licked his lips and gently nipped Aleksi's chin. "Everything."

The bright gold glow in Aleksi's eyes dimmed to leave Aleksi's normal green-yellow stare. "Will you tell me about Garrick, the brother you lost?"

In the back of his mind, he registered Caleb's gasp and the sound of Scott trying to usher his brother away. He'd forgotten that both their brothers were still close enough to overhear.

"Let's go for a ride," Kale suggested.

Aleksi shook his head but Kale grabbed his mate's face and held him still. "I know my body. As long as you go slowly, I'll be fine, but I want to go somewhere peaceful if we're going to spill all these secrets."

The shifter let him move away as Kale sidestepped and turned to Scott and his brother. "We're going to be gone for a while. There's roast beef in the oven and fresh rolls in the bread bin."

Scott grinned and set off for the house, looking as if he would rip apart the kitchen to find the food. One would never know that Scott wasn't a shifter from the way the man shoveled down food. But he supposed when Aleksi and the other bodyguards were regular additions around the dinner table it was eat fast or not eat at all.

Caleb looked taken aback. "You cooked?"

That made Kale laugh, despite the uneasy knots in his stomach. He was the person to admit he had no domestic skills and the first meal he tried to cook in years could have been used as a toxic weapon. He still couldn't figure out how he'd managed to set the beef joint on fire.

"No. I followed directions and mostly passed Aleksi ingredients and plates. Mr. Bossy ran the kitchen like a military operation. There was garlic herb chicken and roasted sweet potatoes too, but we ate that," he replied with a smile and pointed in Aleksi's direction.

"I had to take charge. Otherwise, we'd be stuck eating some squishy green stuff you claim is in all the top restaurants." Aleksi had gotten quicker with comebacks and he liked that he was rubbing off on the powerful man — in more ways than one, anyway.

Kale rolled his eyes. "It was kale. It's healthy."

"That's not what kale tastes like. You're much tastier," Aleksi said in his ear too quietly for Caleb to hear — he hoped.

He made eye contact with his brother and saw the approval there. They'd never told anyone about Garrick. It meant a lot to him that Caleb supported his decision to share their past with Aleksi.

"Go grab some food before Scott eats so much that he won't fit in his suit anymore." Kale nodded reassuringly.

Caleb headed for the house after Scott.

* * * *

Hours later, Kale lay against Aleksi's large, furry side, stroking his fingers through the bristly fur of Aleksi's enormous paws. If someone had told him a month ago that he would be mated to a saber-tooth tiger shifter, sitting with his mate on a cliff edge after telling the man absolutely everything about himself, Kale wouldn't have even given that person a second look. He'd have called a hospital for them.

Aleksi had been mostly silent as he told the shifter about his parents, who had become abusive after

Garrick's death until Caleb was old enough to leave with him and get custody. He'd even told Aleksi about the time he'd considered doing porn to make the rent and buy food but that his first modeling job had come through just in time.

Caleb had been ill with pneumonia and unable to keep his job as an office temp. The cost of medicine had wiped out their meager savings from his after-school job. Kale would have done whatever he had to do, but he was thankful the model recruiter had spotted him before he'd walked through the doors of the film studio. He hadn't expected Aleksi to take that news well but the shifter just growled and rubbed against him, spreading his scent.

The only other time Aleksi had spoken had been to comfort him when Kale had raged at the memory of waiting for Garrick to come home. He also admitted to waking up for weeks after, thinking it had all been a nightmare and that his big brother would skid his motorcycle in over the gravel drive, kicking grit all over the windows.

After a few hours, the sun set and the remaining warmth of the hot day bled away. Kale shivered and snuggled closer to his mate, thinking they should get back soon but not wanting to leave yet.

Aleksi transformed into his human form, then he suggested heading home, but Kale's lack of enthusiasm must have shown. Instead, Aleksi shifted back into his tiger form again and curled around him.

Kale leaned into Aleksi's shoulder and lifted his head to plant a kiss on Aleksi's pink nose. "I love you." He smiled when Aleksi started purring and turned to watch the night birds take to the sky to hunt for their dinners.

Epilogue

George was out of breath by the time he got to the right office building. The men with guns were still following him and he was at his wits end. He didn't know what to do. It wasn't everyday people tried to kill him, blew up his car and sent a hit man to his apartment.

The secretary stopped typing on the computer and greeted him, "Hi, can I help—hey! You can't go in there!" Her voice followed him as she shouted.

"Sorry!" George shouted an over his shoulder. He crashed through the door then took the first left, hoping that there would be someone in the office who could help him.

Somewhere close by, another door opened. Out of the corner of his eye, George saw something very big head down the corridor toward him.

As soon as he entered the office, the man inside talking on a phone dropped the device and shot to his feet. The man started toward George but he was too scared of who or what was behind to turn around now, even if it meant this man would beat him to a pulp.

"Please help me!" He could feel something big and dangerous behind him. He hoped like hell the puff of hot air on the back of his neck was just his imagination.

The man in the suit was drop-dead gorgeous and if he'd met him in a club, George would be on his knees begging the man to take him home so George could do unspeakable things to him. But George's nerves were fried and he was too tired and worn down to do anything about his instant attraction.

George watched, still catching his breath, as the man stopped coming toward him and reached back to pick up the phone he'd dropped on the desk.

"I'll call you back." Then to someone behind George he said, "It's okay. I'll see him. Go back to whatever you were doing, Oscar."

The presence behind him grunted but retreated. George was still too scared to look around to see what or who it had been.

"My *bear* of a friend doesn't like people bursting in without an appointment. I wouldn't advise that you ever repeat this dramatic entrance."

George was grateful the man had called off whatever it was behind him. However, he figured the stunning man's patience and leniency was only going to stretch so far. "The man who kidnapped and hurt that male model was killed yesterday and now there are people trying to kill me." Saying it aloud was too much and he collapsed to his knees, breathing deeply as his hands shook uncontrollably.

The man closed the distance between them and crouched down in front of him.

"Are you talking about Frank George Kelvin, who targeted Kale Andrews?"

"Yes." Hearing about his brother's death had actually been a relief. That model wasn't the first to be victim of Frank's obsessive nature.

"How are you connected to him?"

George swallowed painfully. "He's my brother."

To give the man credit, he didn't flinch. He put firm hands on George's shoulders and shook him gently. "Who is the person trying to kill you?"

His eyes stung. "My father."

This time the man's eyes did flare in surprise, but he quickly smothered his reaction. "My name's Scott and we're going to help you, okay?"

"Thank you." This time George gave in to the need to cry. He sat back on the floor and hoped that the man was right. If not, he probably wouldn't live to see the end of the day.

About the Author

I'm SA Welsh and I write because the voices in my head keep making me. I love reading and I love letting the characters and stories in my head come to life in a book. I can't function in the morning without a cup of tea and when I'm not writing I'm reading. I have enough books to last me through an apocalypse but don't ask me to share them unless you are a fellow book worm and know how to treat and appreciate a good book. It is thanks to the writers that inspired me to put myself out there that I became an author and the editors that make sense of my chaos that I keep writing.

SA Welsh loves to hear from readers. You can find her contact information, website details and author profile page at http://www.totallybound.com.

Totally Bound Publishing

www.ingramcontent.com/pod-product-compliance
Lightning Source LLC
Chambersburg PA
CBHW020420180626
46812CB00003B/1075